·THE DEVIL·
MET A LADY

The Toby Peters Mysteries

-THE DEVIL-
MET A LADY

STUART M. KAMINSKY

®

THE MYSTERIOUS PRESS

Published by Warner Books

A Time Warner Company

Copyright © 1993 by Stuart M. Kaminsky

Mysterious Press books are published by Warner Books, Inc.,
1271 Avenue of the Americas, New York, NY 10020.

A Time Warner Company

The Mysterious Press name and logo are registered trademarks of
Warner Books, Inc.

Printed in the United States of America

First printing: October 1993

10 9 8 7 6 5 4 3 2 1

Library of Congress Cataloging-in-Publication Data

Kaminsky, Stuart M.
    The devil met a lady / Stuart M. Kaminsky.
        p.   cm.
    ISBN 0-89296-436-7
    I. Title.
PS3561.A43D48   1993
813'.54—dc20   92-50659
                                                          CIP

To Luciana Crepax, with thanks for her friendship,
her continuing appreciation of Toby and his misadventures,
and her fantastic translations

·THE DEVIL·
MET A LADY

"You mean all this time we could have been friends?"
Baby Jane to Blanche in *Whatever Happened
to Baby Jane?*

Chapter One

"If I remain in this room for five more minutes, I will surely go mad, mad, mad," Bette Davis said, grabbing the sleeve of my jacket as I reached for the door.

She looked into my eyes. Hers were large and determined. Mine were red and beady.

I couldn't blame her. She'd been holed up in a small room in the Great Palms Hotel on Main for almost twenty-four hours with nothing to eat but room-service ham-and-cheese on white and nothing to drink but water and Ruppert Mellow Light Beer. She had the bed. I had the undersized sofa.

The Great Palms Hotel was a good place to get lost—not in the top twenty-five percent and not in the bottom ten, usually hovering not far from respectable mediocrity.

We were registered as Mr. and Mrs. Giddins, Arthur and Regina Giddins. The names were her choice, just bad enough to be believable, not that the clerk had cared when we checked in at two in the morning. There had been no one in the lobby at that hour, and Davis, wearing a floppy hat that covered most of her face in shadow, had gone immediately, impatiently, with her hip-throwing walk, to a frazzled sofa behind a potted palm. She dropped a nearly empty suitcase in front of her on the floor.

The night clerk's name was Scott Cosacos. It was etched in white on an ebony plate perched on the desk. Scott Cosacos, a thin, pasty, baggy-eyed creature of the night in a wrinkled charcoal-gray suit and no hurry, had glanced at Davis and then at me as we came in. I had done my best, mumbling about fouled-up plane schedules, to draw his attention as she strode across the lobby. There was little for Scott to see, once Davis was seated behind the palm, so he had turned to me.

I was a lot less fun than Bette Davis. Within a few years of fifty, about five-ten, dark brown hair turning gray fast, maybe 175 pounds, with a face that looked as if it had taken fifty punches too many from Tony Zale, I was short of a nightmare and far from a dream.

"Five dollars a night in advance. Check-out's at noon. No exceptions. No questions."

He tried to look over my shoulder at Davis.

"Fine. Late plane from Kansas," I explained as he turned the register around for me to sign.

"None of my business," he said. "Long as you've got luggage and cash."

I signed. He read upside down.

"Room 616, Mr. Giddins," he said. "Want a bellboy?"

"No, wife and I can handle it."

"Then I don't have to wake the bellboy," the clerk said. "And you save yourself a half-buck tip."

"Right," I said, fishing a five from my wallet.

"Logical, Mr. Giddins," he said. "I'm a logical man."

"Admirable in an age of emotion," I countered, with my most winning battered smile. I fished out an extra single and handed it over.

He handed me the key and glanced at Davis again. I

walked over to her wearily, reached down for the suitcases, and let her walk ahead of me to the elevator, keeping myself between her and Cosacos. I did my best to make the suitcase look heavy.

Davis was small, so there was enough of me to block the night clerk's view of her as we crossed the lobby. The elevator, however, was the tricky part. It was open, directly in the clerk's line of sight. He might not recognize her when she turned around, but, with two Academy Awards for best actress and three major films a year, hers was probably the best-known face in the world behind Roosevelt and Hitler.

We couldn't walk up six flights. The vigilant Scott Cosacos would wonder why. And it would look a little odd for the little woman to get on the elevator and stand with her back to the door.

When we got in the elevator I put down the suitcases, stepped toward her, and brought my mouth to hers as she turned. I groped back with my left hand and hit an elevator button. I kept kissing her till I heard the door clank closed behind me and felt the elevator lurch.

She was firm and solid, with full breasts and a mouth as large as it looked on the screen at the Fox. Her breath, through her very slightly parted lips, held the hint of too many cigarettes.

She pushed away from me firmly and I looked down at her pale face.

"Sorry," I said.

"I understand," she replied. "A take."

"For the clerk."

"I prefer rehearsals and a choice of leading men," she said. "But under the circumstances, consider yourself almost forgiven."

Room 616 was small. A single bed, a smaller sofa with a low wooden coffee table in front of it, a sad, unraveling wicker chair, and a little table with a white Arvin radio on top.

I dropped the suitcase on the bed and looked up at a print of a copy of a copy of a painting of the ironclad battleship, *Monitor*. I knew because the name of the ship was stenciled onto its side. The shiny green frame didn't match anything in the room.

The view from the window was better. Main Street. Blackout dark at night. Teaming and steaming with wandering kids in uniform and people of all shapes, shades, ilks, and genders trying to sell or be sold something or someone. When we opened the window we could hear city sounds and smell a nearby Chinese restaurant.

After a minute or two at the window I went to the bathroom, which was small but boasted a fair-sized bathtub and a couple of fairly clean towels.

"Not much," I said.

She was slumped onto the bed, her left arm shielding her eyes from the light—three overhead bulbs covered by pale, yellowed shades.

"What a dump," she said.

"Our choices are limited," I said, opening the suitcase.

She grunted and kept her eyes covered.

She was tired and I was dazed and hungry. I pulled out a pair of pajamas, a book, a razor, and the latest copy of the *Atlantic Monthly*. There wasn't much more in there; there hadn't been time to pack. I'd picked up the suitcase, razor, magazine, and even the pajamas at a late-night drugstore on Olympia Boulevard. Davis had a travel kit with a new Dr. Lyon's toothbrush and powder.

"You want a glass of water?" I asked.

She sat up, looked around as if she had forgotten where we were, got up and took the pajamas from the foot of the bed where I had put them.

"I think I'll just sleep now," she said, heading for the bathroom.

Ten minutes later she turned out the lights and was back in the bed.

"Please close the window," she said.

"Smells and sounds of the city," I said.

"I have worked long days and nights and forgotten about the existence of weekends so that I could afford houses in which I did not have to hear or smell cities."

I closed the window and went into the bathroom. I sat on the edge of the tub reading the *Atlantic Monthly* and wishing I had a bowl of Wheaties, or a glass of milk and a bag of Toll House cookies.

It was close to twenty-four hours later that I announced to Davis that I had to go out for a while, and she announced that she was going mad, mad, mad in the small room of the Great Palms, listening to "The Romance of Helen Trent" on the tinny Arvin.

"Okay," I said, after she had almost calmed down. "I'm going. Bolt the door after me."

"I would prefer to go with you, you know."

"Someone would recognize you."

"Possibly, but it might be worth the risk just to get out of this room," she said, looking around and shuddering.

"The risk is mine, and your husband's too."

"Then," she said, walking me to the door, "I will simply get the sleep I most urgently require."

Six hours later I was back and knocking at the door. I was bruised, limping, and in no mood to talk about it. She opened up after I identified myself, didn't seem to notice my demolished state, and went back to the bed without asking where I'd been.

I didn't volunteer my story then, but I'll fill you in on it . . . a little later. For now I'll tell you that I had found what I was looking for but I paid the price in cracked ribs.

I took off my shirt, locked myself in the bathroom with the *Atlantic*, and poured myself the closest thing the Great Palms could offer to a warm bath to soothe my wounds. I was tired but I knew I snored. Davis had told me she didn't sleep well, that she needed close to total silence. Having had a show of her temper the night before when I didn't even know I was asleep and snoring, I didn't want to wake up in the middle of a second night with Bette Davis standing over me with her hands on her hips. I couldn't shake the memory of that scene in *The Little Foxes*, when she just stood there and let Herbert Marshall die.

I kicked off my shoes, got in the tub. The running water eased my aching legs and I learned from the *Atlantic* that one of President Roosevelt's chief attributes was his "political sagacity"; that, in spite of something called the Baruch Committee Report, the rubber problem was not solved; and that the navy had begun to acknowledge the gravity of the submarine menace.

About two in the morning I hung my trousers on a hook, hitched up my boxer shorts, and turned off the bathroom lights. Then I tiptoed to the sofa, turned away from Bette Davis's gentle snoring, and covered my head with a tiny tasseled pillow.

The next sixteen hours were among the worst in my life and that includes the night I once spent in a cage with a gorilla.

Two nights alone in a hotel room with Bette Davis had driven me to the edge of the cliff of insanity. I was hanging on with my fingertips and wondering if there was any fee I could charge her husband that would make up for this.

Davis did not feel like reading the *Atlantic*. She got bored with the radio by nine in the morning, and conversation did not come easily. She had confiscated my only pair of pajamas half an hour after we had walked into the room, and spent most of her time lounging around smoking or looking out the window with her arms folded and an impatient scowl on her face.

Our conversations consisted of her requests to call her sister, her mother, William Wyler, Geraldine Fitzgerald, and

Howard Hughes. I said no. She insisted. I said no. She got loud.

"At least let me call Farney. He must be worried sick."

Farney, Arthur Farnsworth, was her husband and my client.

I said, "Go ahead and call him. Call 'em all. While you're at it, you might as well call Wiklund and Jeffers and their two wind-up, broken-nosed robots."

"Your nose is also broken," she said triumphantly.

"Smashed flat," I corrected. "I earned it. You want to call your husband or 'G.E. News Time,' go ahead." I pointed to the phone. "Be my guest and the guest of whoever the switchboard operator is downstairs."

"You give in too easily," she said, turning her back on me. "I despise weak men."

"I can't win either way," I observed.

"It is doubtful," she agreed, turning around again.

We glared at each other, trapped animals, wide-eyed, unwilling to blink first. She had more experience with close-ups than I did. I blinked.

She laughed first. I laughed last. The truce lasted about five minutes.

On that second day, I found a battered deck of Bee playing cards in the back of the drawer behind the Gideon Bible. I put cards and Bible on the coffee table near the sofa and asked her to play poker.

"I do not like to play card games," she said. "Card games are designed to kill time. Time should be spent in pleasure or work, not thrown away or murdered."

She had been slowly pacing the floor, wearing the same loose-fitting dark blouse and long dark skirt she had worn the day before, which made sense since that was all she had with her.

"Do you like watching me go nuts?" I asked.

"I don't think so," she said somberly. "Are you going mad?"

"Yes. You?"

"Completely."

"We can talk instead of playing cards," I tried. "Or listen to the radio, or. . ."

"We will play poker," she countered with a sigh as she moved to the sofa next to me. "And you can listen to the radio."

I turned on the little white hotel Arvin and a deep voice said, ". . . Russian troops thirty miles from Rostov."

"Music only," she ordered, pushing the battered deck of cards toward me on the coffee table.

I spun the dial and changed stations till I found Helen Forrest singing "I've Heard That Song Before."

"You got any money with you?" I asked as I dealt the cards.

"Yes, but I do not bet money."

"You've got money in the stock market?"

"No."

"Real estate?"

"I have my house in Glendale, which I use when I am working; Butternut, my house in New Hampshire. I pay for my mother's house and my sister's nervous breakdowns. I have many expenses and a few investments," she said. "And I do not consider owning a home a gamble in real estate."

I considered making small talk about Glendale, since my brother and I both grew up there. I didn't consider it long or hard.

"All right," I tried instead. "What will we play for if not money?"

"If that is meant to be risqué, I am not, under the present circumstances, interested in crude or even remarkably adroit jokes of a sexual nature," she said. "Do we look at the cards?"

"Yes."

She picked up the cards and fanned them awkwardly.

"That does not mean, however, that a situation might not

arise in which I might well be interested in crude jokes of a sexual nature. What is the point of this game?"

"Highest hand wins," I said.

"Highest hand wins?"

"Best cards. The most of something."

I had three sixes.

"Yes," she said.

"How many cards do you want?"

She looked at her cards forever.

"This is just to teach you," I said. "You can get rid of any cards you don't want."

"I don't want any cards," she said.

"I'll take two."

I came up with another six and a king.

"Now, if we were betting..."

"But we are not," she reminded me.

"What have you got?"

I spread my four sixes and a king before her. She followed my lead. She didn't even have a pair.

"Who has the higher?" she asked.

"Guess."

She stared at the cards and then looked up at me. She rested her head on her right hand and examined the cards once more.

"What does it matter?"

"If we were betting, it would matter," I said.

"I have greater variety," she pointed out correctly. "More numbers and all four suits."

"I have four sixes."

"Ah, now I understand. In poker, unlike other sources of entertainment, repetition is better than variety," she said, opening her eyes wide and looking at me with a smile.

I put the cards away and let Helen Forrest finish before I announced that I intended to go to sleep at nine.

"I promise not to snore if you promise not to snore," I said.

She didn't bother to answer that one.

The highlight of this second day in hell, for me, anyway, was going to the Beau Jack–Fritzie Zivic fight from Madison Square Garden, which would be coming on the radio in about an hour. Or maybe I'd switch back and forth between stations and listen to the Ray (Sugar) Robinson–Jake LaMotta bout too. Robinson hadn't lost in one hundred and thirty straight fights. It figured to be less interesting than the Jack-Zivic bout.

I'd been out twice the day before to make my calls and run my late-night errand. I'd also be out once this morning. Now I had to make another trek to the lobby. There was a phone in the room, but the hotel operator might listen in and hear something that would get us in trouble.

"I'm going with you," she said.

"Come on. You know someone will recognize you," I said. "When we checked in, that clerk..."

"All right," she said, letting go of my jacket. "All right. Yes. What you say makes perfect sense, but..."

Her shoulders slumped, her chin came up, her eyes filled with tears.

"Go," she said, her voice breaking.

"You did that in *Now, Voyager*," I said.

The tears disappeared. Her lips tightened and she kicked me in the shins.

"*The Bride Came C.O.D.*," I said.

"How comforting to be entombed with a fan," she said, opening the door for me. "It could, however, be worse. At least you are not Miriam Hopkins."

I opened my mouth to speak, but she interrupted with, "Do not tell me which of my films that was from. Leave me at least minimally confident that I created one line without the aid of a Warner Brothers writer."

"I was just going to say, lock the door behind me."

"Try to find some Graham crackers," she said. "And one more thing. I've been playing poker since I was six."

I went out without looking back. The door clicked locked. I had no elaborate plan. Go to the lobby. Make a couple of calls in the hope that the people who were trying to kidnap Davis had been found. Pick up a couple of nonhotel sandwiches, maybe even some tacos and a couple of Pepsi's. Hell, the night was young. Maybe I'd find a box of cereal, a carton of milk, and some cookies. Breathe free.

I made it as far as the lobby and the phone. The lobby was full, not crowded but full. A quartet of middle-aged salesmen in last year's suits, a pair of preteen sailors talking to a woman who was old enough to be their high-school music teacher and experienced enough to teach them how to play an instrument of their choice, assorted couples, singles, check-ins and check-outs. I was dropping my nickel in the slot when I saw them.

There were three of them: Hans and Fritz, both big, one blond, one dark; one broad, the other lean. Hans was broad and blond. Fritz was smaller but meaner. I ought to know. He had tried to skewer me with a fencepost two nights before. The third stooge, Jeffers, short, nervous, with slicked-back dark hair and a nose that pointed a little to the left, was talking to the desk clerk.

I turned my back when Fritz started to scan the crowd, but before I turned I saw what I didn't want to see—Scott Cosacos, the logical night clerk, was just coming on duty, relieving the slightly more savory-looking younger man with no hair, who was talking to Jeffers.

When the telephone operator came on, I told her I'd changed my mind, hung up, and made it to the stairs, hiding behind a pair of salesmen talking about friction bolts, a trio of teenage sailors arguing about beer, a weary lady of the afternoon, and a family of five who looked like they were on vacation from Moline, Illinois.

On the stairway, I turned around carefully and saw Jeffers watching Scott Cosacos, whose eyes lifted over their heads and moved around the crowd. I pressed against the wall and hurried upward.

Going up was not easy. I have a bad back and my leg was recovering from a not-distant break of major proportions. On top of that there were the wounds of the previous two nights.

"You didn't get the Graham crackers," Bette Davis observed from the table where she was smoking and staring at the cards.

"We're going," I said, throwing things into the suitcase. "They're downstairs."

"No," she said, standing.

"Yes," I said, throwing the cards into the case and snapping it shut. "Put your shoes on."

She obeyed quickly.

"One more time," I said, hoisting the suitcase. "Maybe it's time we went to the police."

"No," she said. "There will be pictures, photographers, stories. And Farney has specifically. . ."

"Hans and Fritz could kill us. That might be a little more inconvenient than the police."

I was at the door now, opening it slightly.

"No police."

"Okay, then," I whispered, ushering her out into the hall. "Let's go."

The hallway was empty. My .38 was tucked in my belt.

Stairs or elevator. I figured there were no odds on Cosacos not telling Jeffers, Hans, and Fritz where Mr. and Mrs. Giddins were.

"Stairs," I said, though my leg and back said elevator.

She followed. Less than a flight down I heard footsteps coming up. Could be anyone looking for exercise. Could be. I motioned for her to follow me back upstairs. On the sixth floor I pushed the elevator button as I watched the stairwell.

Five, ten seconds. Twenty. The elevator clicked into place and the doors started to open as Fritz came into view, taking the last two or three stairs in one stride. There was something in his hand.

"In, fast," I said, shoving Davis into the elevator. She didn't move. I shoved her again. Still she didn't move. And then I looked. Hans and Jeffers were standing against the rear wall of the elevator. Hans had his arms folded, which would have been a good sign if Jeffers hadn't had a pistol in his hand.

I considered our options.

Hans reached forward and held the elevator door open as Jeffers said, "Step in, put your suitcase slowly on the floor, hand me your gun, and turn around."

Fritz was behind us now, blocking our way if we stupidly decided to run for the stairs.

"Now, see here," Bette Davis said indignantly. "We are not getting in your elevator. We are not going with you. If you do not leave immediately, I will scream, a scream such as you have never even imagined. You have no intention of shooting us and we have no intention of coming with you. I've seen as much of you as I intend to see. So take your two-bit gangster act and sell it to Monogram."

The elevator door began to rattle, anxious to respond to calls above and below.

"You are one hell of a great actress, lady," Jeffers said with a smile. "We'll have plenty of time for your next performance when we get where we're going. Now, I am going to count to three—then, if you are not on this elevator, I will shoot Mr. Peters. My colleague will restrain and gag you and carry you down the service stairs to an automobile waiting at the service entrance."

"I don't think so," said Davis, looking at me and then Jeffers with a confident smile.

"One," said Jeffers.

The elevator door begged to close.

"Two," he said.

Hans and Fritz waited patiently, Fritz standing directly behind Bette Davis.

"Get in," I said to her.

"He is bluffing," she said.

"I don't think so," I said.

Jeffers cocked his head to one side and aimed his revolver at my head. Fritz moved a little to his left to avoid the splatter of blood.

"All right," said Davis with a sigh.

Jeffers lowered the gun, and Fritz ushered the two of us into the elevator. The doors closed in relief and we began to go down.

"God, what a moment," said Jeffers. "A scene with Bette Davis. If that jackass of an agent of mine could have seen me. I was good, wasn't I?"

"Walter Brennan is shivering in fright from the threat you pose to his career," she said.

"She's amazing," said Jeffers to Hans, who stood stone-faced. "Amazing," he repeated, looking at me as the elevator slowed down.

"Amazing," I agreed.

"He was bluffing," Bette Davis said.

"No," said Jeffers soberly. "I wasn't. And I'll shoot you both and whoever gets on this elevator if you pull anything."

"Your dialogue is deteriorating," she said as the elevator doors opened slowly on the third floor and an ancient couple dressed in their Iowa-farm best got on and glared at us.

"Slowest damned elevator I've ever seen," the man said accusingly.

Jeffers smiled and nodded agreement. The sight of Jeffers, me, and the Katzenjammer Kids was enough to silence the old woman, who faced front stoically. The old man, who wore glasses, a gray suit, and a scowl, looked at Bette Davis, blinked and turned front also.

When we reached the lobby, the door clanked open and the old couple stepped out. The man whispered something and the twig-thin old woman looked back at us as Fritz urged us toward the front door.

"Nonsense," the old woman whispered. "She doesn't look anything like Joan Crawford."

And as we wove our way through the lobby crowd with Jeffers's buddy-buddy arm around my shoulder, his pistol under my jacket pressed into my spine, Bette Davis uttered, "Is there no end to the humiliation I must endure?"

I didn't answer but I felt like saying that humiliation was not in the same class with what I was sure Jeffers planned for me when he got us somewhere away from Joan Crawford's admiring fans.

Chapter Two

Let's go back a little. Not long and not far, only three days and a few blocks from the Great Palms Hotel. On Monday, February 1, 1943, I was sitting in my office on the fourth floor of the Farraday Building on Hoover and Ninth, a few doors down from Manny's Tacos.

My office is my private domain, monk's cell, my refuge or, as Bette Davis might observe, a dump. Few ever enter the office of Toby Peters, Private Investigator, especially clients. Aside from me, only a cat named Dash, a fat orange lump who belongs to no one but lives with me, spends a lot of time there. Sheldon Minck, the dentist with whom I share the suite, is permitted to bring me announcements of visitors; Jeremy Butler, who owns the Farraday and is an enormous ex-wrestler who lives on the floor above us with his wife and new daughter, can enter whenever he wishes.

There are those who might say that I keep clients away from my office because it is little more than a closet inside the less-than-clean disaster of a dental surgery where Shelly practices incompetent alchemy and benevolent sadism. There are those who might say that my office, which smells like a fat orange cat, is unimpressive: a small cluttered and battered desk; a single window five stories above an alley where a bum who keeps changing his name resides in the rusting shell of a Buick; a cracked ceiling; barely enough room for two wooden chairs beside my own; a bleary blown-up photograph on the wall of me, my brother Phil, our father wearing his grocer's apron, and our dog Kaiser Wilhelm.

And there are those who might wonder at the strange painting that covers one entire wall, the painting of a woman lovingly cradling two small naked boy babies. Someone might think the woman was my mother, and the boy babies me and my brother Phil. In fact, they were Salvador Dali, his dead brother, and his mother, who was still alive as far as I knew. Dali had given me the painting as payment for a job I had done for him.

There are those who might say many things about the office of Toby Peters, Private Investigator, if they had the interest or opportunity.

On Monday, I was blissfully, ignorantly, and unaccountably content. Nothing in my life, outside of having enough money to pay my overdue bills, accounted for this feeling.

Sure, the war news was good. The *Los Angeles Times* front page told me that Nazi Stalingrad Chief Field Marshal General Friedrich von Paulus and sixteen other generals had been captured by the Russians, and that the Germans had suffered their worst defeat of the war, one hundred thousand men killed. And there, right in front of me, was the announcement that Secretary of the Navy Frank Knox had just returned from a two-week tour of the Pacific, saying the Japanese resistance on Guadalcanal would end in thirty days.

I had forty dollars in my wallet and another three hundred in my only other pair of shoes, in a closet at Mrs. Plaut's boarding house, where I lived. The money was in payment for a case I handled for Greta Garbo in one day. The fee was only two hundred bucks. The extra hundred and forty was a bonus to insure my promise that I wouldn't tell anyone what had happened, ever. I had told her the bonus wasn't necessary. She had insisted. I had held out for five whole seconds.

Those who seek my services through former clients, friends, acquaintances, and ex-wives have learned that I don't sell brilliant deductions and a vast network of contacts in high places. What I do sell is dogged persistence, confidentiality, and a face that had once been described by Peter Lorre as "classic expressionism."

As a result, I'm frequently looking for part-time jobs, hanging around Levy's restaurant on Spring Street trying to seduce Carmen the cashier into a romantic nightlife of cowboy movies and hot-dog stands on the beach. When not pursuing the ample Carmen, I prowl after the even more elusive Anne Mitzenmacher, my former wife who divorced me half-a-dozen years and a few thousand busted promises ago. My brother, who's an L.A. Police captain, has no use for me, and I have some very lonely days and some damned good ones. This Monday was a damned good one.

If I wanted to work, which I didn't, since I was sitting on the vast wealth I had earned from Garbo, I could have done a night house-detective stint at any of five downtown hotels. No, I was preparing to go down to Levy's restaurant and boldly invite Carmen to join me for a few days in Lake Tahoe. Maybe she would accept. Maybe she would let me pay for a sitter so her twelve-year-old son didn't have to join us. Maybe she would utter more than a few weary words and display something beyond complete, widemouthed indifference.

"Have you noticed," I told Dash, who had been nibbling at an open envelope containing an invitation to join the Vegetarian Party, "that my vocabulary has improved as a result of my association with Jeremy?"

Dash didn't give a rat's tail. He kept munching.

"The key to success is convincing the world that you went to a school east of Denver," I told Dash.

Dash looked up with a strip of envelope flap glued to his nose. I reached over and removed it.

The phone rang. I picked it up.

"Toby Peters Agency," I said, dropping my voice a few decibels to client-confidence level. With potential clients I was a baritone, at least for the first day.

"My name is Arthur Farnsworth," the man said in a back-East voice that suggested a good education or a top-notch language coach. "I've been told you might be able to help me."

"Mr. Farnsworth," I said. "I'm afraid you caught me at a bad time. I'm about to go on vacation. If your case can wait a week, I'll be happy to talk. If it can't, I can recommend—"

"No," Farnsworth shouted loud enough to make Dash look up from his tasty envelope. "This is very important and the person who recommended you said no one else would do."

"Look—" I began.

"National security is involved here, Mr. Peters," he said. "Give me five minutes of your time. I'll come right over."

"No," I said. "I'll tell you what. I was on my way out for lunch. You know Levy's Grill on Spring Street?"

"Yes," he said.

"Can you make it in fifteen minutes?"

"Twenty-five," he said.

"Twenty-five," I agreed. "Just ask the cashier who I am."

I hung up the phone and didn't bother to check the watch on my wrist. The watch had belonged to my father. I got it when he died. It was the only thing I got from him besides vague memories and a lopsided grin. The watch had refused, in the more than three decades I'd had it, to simply quit. It also refused to come close to the right time. I loved that watch. It reminded me of me.

"You want to come with me or stay here?" I asked Dash.

He looked up from the confettied envelope and blinked a couple of times.

"Why don't you come with me?" I said, picking him up.

"Shelly'll probably forget to feed you. You can eat what's left of the upholstery in my car."

This seemed a good idea to Dash. At least he didn't protest.

The phone rang. I debated answering. I didn't have much time to make it to Levy's, charm Carmen, order a Levy's Patriotic Reuben—with Kraft cheese and coleslaw instead of Swiss and sauerkraut—and be ready for Farnsworth of the East.

I picked up the phone.

"Mr. Peelers?" blasted the voice of my ancient landlady, Mrs. Plaut.

I put the receiver down on the desk. There was no point in telling Mrs. Plaut that I had to hurry to meet a potential client, or even that the Farraday Building was surrounded by savage Eskimos. I had learned through hard and painful experience that the only way to deal with Mrs. Plaut was to hear her out and, if at all possible, obey. Any other path led to a labyrinth of confusion, apology, and failure. Occasionally, and to my deep regret, I sometimes forgot this simple truth.

"It's me, Mrs. Plaut."

"It is you," she shouted.

"It is."

"Good. It is necessary for you to stop at Ralph's Market," she said. "Please get your pencil."

I put Dash back down on the desk, pulled the notebook out of my rear pocket, and found a pencil on the desk.

"Ready," I said.

"Are you prepared?"

"I am prepared."

Though she was nearly deaf, Mrs. Plaut heard reasonably well on the telephone. The problem was that she assumed others couldn't hear unless she helped the sound along the wires by shouting. I wrote dutifully as she made her way carefully through the list.

"A big box of Climalene. Two Waldorf toilet tissues. Pay no

more than a nickel for each. A jar of Musterole. A box of French's Birdseed, for Dexter. The kind Virginia Bruce gives her canary. A box of Aunt Jemima Ready-Mix Pancakes. An Arrid Cream Deodorant. The thirty-nine-cent jar, not the ten-cent or the fifty-nine-cent one. One pound of Durkee's Vegetable Oleomargarine. A jar of Spry. Four cans of Prem. That's Prem, not Spam. Last time you brought Spam. Spam is not sugar-cured."

"I understand."

"And a Silvercup bread. And a milk. And, Mr. Peelers, I must remind you that U.S. Government wartime milk regulations go into effect today," she said.

"Yes," I said neutrally.

"There will be a three-cent deposit on the store bottle. The radio says that half a million bottles a year are not returned. These bottles are needed for the war effort."

"Thank you for the information," I said.

"There is a point to my conveying this information to you, Mr. Peelers."

"I never doubted it, Mrs. Plaut."

"You are using a milk bottle in your room for a penny bank and another for a flowerpot. You have forty-two pennies in that bank and have not added one in many months. The flower in your milk bottle died more than a month ago."

"Take the bottles, Mrs. Plaut," I said.

"Good. I'll reimburse you for the groceries when I check them. Do not be late."

With that she hung up. I did the same, tucked my notebook into my back pocket, reached down, swooping a dazed Dash under my arm, and headed for the door, where I almost ran into Jeremy Butler.

Jeremy was massive, bald, and somewhere in his mid-sixties. He was wearing a gray long-sleeved sweat shirt and dark pants. Jeremy owned at least three buildings, including the Farraday. He managed and kept them with his wife, Alice Pallis, who almost matched him in bulk and strength.

He also found time to write and publish poetry and to engage in adoration of his and Alice's baby, Natasha, a beauty whose existence belied her heredity.

"On the way out," I said. "Client."

"I won't keep you," said Jeremy. "Did you hear the news?"

"Stalingrad," I said, moving past him.

"No," he said seriously. "Edna St. Vincent Millay received the Medal of the Poetry Society of America in New York. Alice and I are holding a small party tonight in her honor. We'll have readings from *The Murder of Lidice* and some sonnets. I'm also composing a brief poem in her honor."

"I'll do my best to be there," I said. "Will you do me a favor?"

Jeremy said nothing.

"Take care of Dash for a while."

Jeremy took the docile cat.

"Thanks."

"Pick him up at the celebration," said Jeremy. "Our apartment. Nine o'clock."

"Nine o'clock," I repeated, and headed for the door.

The lights were on and bright in Shelly's chamber of horrors, but he wasn't in sight. The patient chair was occupied only by the oversized plaster model of a set of teeth which Shelly used to demonstrate how to brush properly. The plaster teeth were yellow, dirty, and beyond cleaning with anything less than a blowtorch.

The sink in the corner was, as always, filled with dishes. The trash container was, as always, flowing over with unsavory, used cloth pads and cotton swabs.

I pleaded with my back not to go out on me as I hurried six flights down the stairway of the Farraday. I had no time for the elevator.

My footsteps echoed, and wordless voices sang, argued, screamed, and guffawed behind each door. The tenants of the Farraday included bookies, alcoholic physicians, baby photographers with astigmatism, a fortune-teller named Juanita, at least three talent agents, and a long list of con artists who were long on con and short on artistry. In the lobby, I was greeted by the satisfying smell of Lysol, which Jeremy and Alice used in bulk vats to hold off the alternative.

About twenty minutes later I entered Levy's on Spring at the crack of noon. The tables were full of people on their lunch break, taking advantage of the sixty-five-cent special, eating fast and talking loud.

Carmen looked up from giving change to a pale man in a three-piece suit whose shoulders swayed as if he were listening to some internal tune. The man looked a little like Donald Meek, the whiskey drummer in *Stagecoach*.

"Toby," she said. "He's here. Back table near the kitchen."

"Farnsworth?" I asked.

"Yes," she said with more enthusiasm than I'd heard from her since I took her to see Man Mountain Dean and Ruffy Silverstein wrestle two years before at the Olympic.

She handed the dancer his change and he bopped out, giving way to a corn-blond couple in their thirties who could have been twins or married. I squinted toward the table near the kitchen. A guy about forty with a round handsome face and straight brown hair was playing with his coffee and looking back at me.

"Should I know him?" I asked Carmen, nodding at Farnsworth.

"He's married to Bette Davis," she whispered.

The blond couple adjusted their glasses in unison and turned to look at Arthur Farnsworth, who nervously adjusted his tie.

"Client," I said. "I'll tell you about it later."

I moved around the tables, enjoying the smells of Levy's, and made my way to Farnsworth, who stood up to greet me. He was wearing a leather jacket and blue denim pants, all new. He was also wearing a worried look and the faint smell of Sen-Sen. Standing up, he was shorter than I had expected, and heavier, an ex–college lineman.

"Peters?" he asked, holding out his hand.

I took the hand. Grip firm. Face serious. Breath 80 proof beyond the Sen-Sen.

"Farnsworth," I said.

We sat and I motioned for Rusty the waiter. Rusty, so named because he was born ancient and arthritic, creaked his way toward us.

"Thanks for coming," Farnsworth said, lighting a cigarette. "I know you're not really interested, but someone—"

"Someone?" I asked as Rusty made it to our table. He was short, thin, corroded, and raspy.

"What'll it be?" he demanded.

"American Reuben and a Pepsi for me," I said, raising an eyebrow at Farnsworth, who glanced at his coffee.

"Just coffee," he said.

Rusty grunted. The trip had hardly been worth the pain. He turned and left us.

"Someone told you to come to me," I reminded him.

"Oh, yes. Let me explain. My wife is—"

"Bette Davis," I said casually above a roar of laughter from one of the four men at the table behind us.

"You do your research," said Farnsworth.

"My job," I said with a shrug.

"I'll come to the point," he said, leaning over the table toward me and lowering his voice, though no one was listening to us and only Carmen across the room at the cash register was glancing our way. "Someone is threatening me, suggesting that he'll create a scandal, hinting that he'll kidnap my wife, claiming they have something that will ruin her career."

"Go to the police," I said.

He shook his head.

"Then pay him."

"No, it's not like that. And they don't want money. If I go

to the police the newspapers will find out, the radio, the fan magazines. And the police can't watch her all the time. They'll assign someone for a week or two. We'll get a lot of publicity and, besides, I'd have to tell the police why someone threatened Bette or wanted her kidnapped. I can't do that."

"Why?"

"Because," he went on, "I'm involved in some very private aeronautical research. I'm a pilot and . . . I can't say much more. My work is done very quietly in Minnesota for a nongovernment research company. If we're successful, the war could end sooner than we hoped. Obviously, there are people who know a little about what we're doing who don't want us to succeed."

"Spies."

He shrugged. "Spies, Nazi sympathizers."

"What makes you think? . . ."

"I told you. I got a phone call," said Farnsworth, putting out his cigarette and lighting another as Rusty returned with my sandwich and Pepsi. He gave Farnsworth a disgusted look and dropped the check between us.

Farnsworth waited till Rusty was moving to another table before he went on. "The man said he had something that my wife and I would not want to get into the hands of the wrong people. Some nonsense about a record of my wife and her first husband. He indicated that I might want to trade some information on the work I was doing for the recording. He said that if I didn't see him to discuss it, my wife might disappear and the record might be sent to the newspapers. He also said I shouldn't tell anyone."

"You're telling me," I said, lifting half the American Reuben in two hands and taking a bite.

"The man on the phone told me to call you," he said.

"Me?"

"The man on the phone said you were the person to act as a go-between to arrange delivery of the papers they want. He said you would know he was telling the truth about the record." Farnsworth looked decidedly nervous and fingered his coffee cup. "Peters, I don't know if you're involved in this or not and I don't care, but you've got to protect my wife and you've got to convince this person that I cannot give him those plans."

"Why believe this guy on the phone?" I asked, nibbling at a few crumbs I had missed.

"He . . . he played part of a record of Bette's voice. She was saying . . . saying . . ."

"Forget it," I stopped him. "I don't have to know." I was beginning to get the eyes-in-the-back-of-my-head feeling that I was being set up.

"If I tell the people I work for about this," Farnsworth said, "they'll want to pull Bette from Los Angeles, hide her someplace. She won't do it. She has to work. And even if they go to the government and they do assign some people to watch her, we'll have the publicity problem again."

I grunted and kept eating.

"And there's one more problem," he went on. "I'm not sure the people I work for or the police would believe me. They might think it was a publicity stunt. This is Hollywood. People do things like that all the time."

"I know," I said, finishing a mouthful, "but that's not the reason they wouldn't believe you."

Farnsworth took a deep breath and shook his head.

"Cops and G-men might think the phone call and kidnapping threat came out of a bottle," I concluded.

"Yes, I have a drinking problem," he said. "I've been trying to deal with it. I don't think Bette knows how bad it is, but the people I work for do, and you're right. I doubt if it would take the police long to find out. I'm good at what I do, but . . . I got that call, Mr. Peters. I've been honest with you. I've told you more than I've even told my wife. I'm desperate. He told me they'd contact you, that I had to persuade you to do this for me. He was so sure you'd do it."

I drank some Pepsi and tried to ignore Carmen's broad smile and ample breasts, which were now somehow suggestively visible in the curve of her white blouse.

"Twenty-five a day plus expenses," I said. "To protect your wife, possibly to find out who this person is. If it's some crackpot, fine, but... Can you pick that up for a week or two?"

"I think so," he said. "Then you accept?"

"I want to think about it a while."

"There isn't time to think about it," Farnsworth said nervously. "The man who called said I had no more than a day to find you and be ready to give him an answer."

"Can I finish my sandwich and drink?" I asked.

"Sure."

"You don't think this guy is just a nut," I said.

Farnsworth shook his head.

"Why?"

Arthur Farnsworth looked toward the window of Levy's, just beyond Carmen. She caught the look, thought it was thrown at her, and grinned.

"He sounded sane and I told you he played me part of the record on the phone," he said, looking at me again. "Maybe it was a fake, but... it would ruin Bette's career."

I forked up stray bits of corned beef and coleslaw and we didn't do any more talking for about three minutes. When I was finished, I reached out my right hand and he took it.

"Deal," I said. "I keep good records and bill you as soon as the job is done, or monthly, if it goes that long. I need two hundred in advance."

Farnsworth happily dug into his pocket for his wallet and came up with the right number of twenty-dollar bills.

"You want a receipt?" I asked.

"No," he said. "You'll start today?"

"I'll start today," I agreed. "Let's go talk to your wife."

I reached for the check Rusty had dropped on the table.

Farnsworth's mind was somewhere else; he didn't stop me. Fine. He'd get a bill for it. I got up, check in hand.

"That's a problem," said Farnsworth, getting up. "I mean, talking to Bette."

"Why?"

"I'd rather she not know about this," he said. "I don't want to frighten her.'"

"I'm supposed to protect her without her knowing it?"

"Yes," he said.

"Won't work, Arthur," I said, getting familiar. "She'll spot me within a few days. If I'm supposed to keep people from grabbing her in your house or on the street, I've got to be close. And with this face, I can't just melt into a crowd of fans."

Actually, there was almost no way Bette Davis would fail to spot me. My face was not unfamiliar to her. We'd both spent a good part of our life sentence at Warner Brothers, she as a well-paid slave, me as a badly paid guard.

"Try," he said earnestly, moving inches from my face and taking a firm grip on my right arm. "Please."

"Three conditions," I said. "One, if I have to, I can tell her what's going on. I'd rather have you do it and I'll try to reach you if I can, but I want your okay."

"You've got it," he said. "Here's my card with two numbers where you can reach me. I've written our home number on the back."

"Second condition," I went on. "If this guy does contact me, I want your okay to tell him whatever I want."

"Lie, promise, do whatever you have to," he said. "Just stop him and take care of Bette. The last condition?"

I liked Arthur Farnsworth. He was an easy client. "I may need to use some associates. I'll pay them out of my fee. If you have some reason to meet them, I don't want to hear any complaints."

"You're the professional," he said. "I have no intention of questioning your choice of associates."

"One is a bald giant. Another is a little person, about three feet tall. The last, who I use only in emergencies, is a short, fat guy with thick glasses and a built-in cigar."

"You're joking," Farnsworth said as Rusty squeezed past us to pick up his tip. I'd been generous. Rusty looked as close to happy as he could get.

"They're invaluable," I said. "The bad guys always underestimate them."

Farnsworth now looked a bit less sure of himself and his choice, but it was a done deal.

"Bette's doing a radio show tonight," Farnsworth said. "Screen Guild play, *Dodsworth*, with Walter Huston. She just finished shooting a new movie, *Old Acquaintance*, with Miriam Hopkins. I warn you, Bette's a little frazzled. Miriam is not one of her favorite people and she's still having trouble with her Warners contract."

"Used to work for Warners," I said as we moved toward the grinning Carmen.

"You did?"

"Security," I said. "Got fired by Jack Warner in person for punching a cowboy star who was pawing a wardrobe girl."

"You and Bette have something in common," Farnsworth said with a sad smile as I handed the check and a five-dollar bill to Carmen.

More than you'd think, I said, but only to myself.

"Your wife is my favorite actress, Mr. Davis," Carmen blurted at Farnsworth. "Ask Toby."

"It's true," I said, waiting for my change. Carmen's favorite actor or actress changed every three to six weeks. Buck Jones held the six-week record.

"Thank you," said Farnsworth uncomfortably.

"My change, Carmen," I reminded her, my hand still out. Carmen rang it up and handed the coins to Farnsworth with a smile. He dropped them into my open palm.

"I've got some work to do for Mr. Davis," I said, leaning

over to whisper to Carmen. "But when I finish, maybe you and I could take a much-needed vacation."

Carmen looked at me, her large dark eyes alert for a trap, her wide red mouth ready for an ambush. Farnsworth had discreetly taken a step away from the counter to give us privacy.

"We'll see," she said.

"Tahoe," I said.

"I'll think on it," she said, her eyes back on Farnsworth.

Farnsworth and I headed for the door. I held it open for him. "I'll start tonight," I said. "If that guy calls you back, let me know. If we need it, I've got some connections in the Los Angeles Police Department. My brother's a captain. Need a ride?" I asked.

"No, thanks," he said, looking up and down the street. "I'm parked nearby and I have a few things to do before I head home."

I uncharitably suspected that one of the things was to go to a bar and drink his lunch. We shook again and I said, "Call me if you hear and I'll let you know if I have anything to report."

Chapter Three

Mrs. Plaut's boarding house, which I had called home for more than two years, was in Hollywood on Heliotrope in a reasonably quiet residential neighborhood of small homes, three-floor apartment buildings, and boarding houses.

I arrived, a brown paper bag of groceries in each arm, around two in the afternoon. Mrs. Plaut sat waiting on the porch in her white wicker chair, a bowl of something in her lap which she was mashing with a vengeful wooden spoon. Her radio was plugged in behind her and entertaining the neighborhood with what I think was a soap opera, probably "Rosemary."

Mrs. Plaut was a gray wisp of a woman, tiny, determined, hard of hearing, resolute of purpose, and of no known age. Her white hair was a mass of tight curls and her eyes a pale blue. Mrs. Plaut believed, alternatively, that I was either an exterminator with unsavory friends or a book editor. With the latter forever in her hopes, I was in the process of editing Mrs. Plaut's family history, a tome which was now to be measured not by pages but by pounds. I had considered trying to convince her to stop writing simply to keep from wasting paper that might contribute substantially to the war effort.

"Good afternoon, Mr. Peelers," she said, looking at the packages.

"Good afternoon, Mrs. Plaut," I answered.

"I have been waiting for you for several hours," she said, reaching back to turn off the radio, "and I am browned off."

"Browned off?" I repeated, stepping across the white wooden porch to the front door.

"Bored," she explained. "I heard it on the Arthur Godfrey radio show in the morning. Army bomber lingo. Like laying the eggs."

"Dropping bombs?" I guessed.

She nodded in confirmation. I hadn't gone to UCLA for two years for nothing.

"Can I put these in your kitchen?" I asked.

"Just put those in the kitchen," she said. "I'm making gumbatz. I can't stop or it'll close up."

"I wouldn't want that to happen," I said, and managed to get a hand loose to open the door.

"Don't let Dexter see the box of b-i-r-d-s-e-e-d," she spelled in a whisper.

Mrs. Plaut was a firm believer in the secrecy of spelling. It kept not only children and birds from understanding you, but also adults who seemed to turn into children or birds in the presence of Mrs. Plaut. She had been known to engage in secret spelling in the presence of my friend and fellow boarder, Gunther Wherthman. Now, Gunther may be less than a yard high, but he is over forty and speaks six languages fluently.

"I won't," I whispered, and headed through the open door to Mrs. Plaut's downstairs rooms.

Mrs. Plaut's living room, which she called her sitting room, was overstuffed and doilied. A bird cage holding Dexter stood near the window. Dexter hopped around a

little, looked in my direction with his head cocked—probably
to be sure I didn't have Dash with me—and began chirping
to himself.

In Mrs. Plaut's kitchen I placed the bags on the table,
fished out my milk, coffee, bananas, Rice Krispies, Wheaties,
and Hydrox cream-filled cookies. I cradled them awkwardly
in my arms and set back out for the hallway in the hope that
I could make it up the stairs and to my room before Mrs.
Plaut completed mashing her gumbatz and came up with
another chore for me.

I didn't make it. I almost never make it. She stood
blocking her doorway, bowl in one hand, wooden spoon in
the other. The spoon pointed at me, accusingly.

"You have not returned my last chapter," she said. "The
one about Grandma Teller and the peddler."

"I'll have it back soon," I said. "I'm on a very important
job, government, top secret."

"Tomorrow will be fine," she said. "I have removed your
rent from the shoe in your closet."

"You are a considerate woman," I said, feeling the bottle
of milk starting to slide through my fingers. "Now, if—"

"And I've taken the milk bottles you were hoarding."

"Thanks."

"But not your pennies."

"Thank you."

"I suggest you stop chatting and get up to your room
before you drop that milk."

She stepped out of the way and let me pass. I made my
way up the stairs, moving slowly, fearing the shattering loss
of milk. No milk, no cereal, nothing to dip my Hydrox
cookies in.

I made it to my room and pushed open the door. It wasn't
locked. There was no point in locking it against Mrs. Plaut,
who had a passkey and to whom privacy was a sin. I trusted
the other tenants. At the moment, there were just three of
us: me, Mr. Hill the mailman who got drunk every New

Year's and sang at Mrs. Plaut's party, and Gunther. Gunther had the room next to mine where he worked translating technical documents, reports, and occasionally fiction into English from the languages he spoke and read.

Gunther was the best-dressed man of any size I have ever met. Gunther was the essence of dignity. Gunther was now also in love and seldom in the room next to mine, where he should have been working.

The object of Gunther's affection was a toothpick of a graduate student in art history from San Francisco. Her name was Gwen. Gwen was serious, scholarly, and almost two feet taller than Gunther. They were inseparable. Since it made Gunther happy, I hoped they stayed that way.

I dropped my groceries on the bed in the corner. Each night, when I slept at home, I pulled the mattress to the floor to keep it firm under my tender back. The first time my back had gone out had been at a movie premiere when a large Negro gentleman had given me an unfriendly hug. I was moonlighting for M.G.M., trying to protect Mickey Rooney from his fans. This fan had been more determined than the rest.

The sun was high and my room bright. I looked around. The Beech-Nut Gum clock was keeping reasonable time on the wall over my dresser. The pillow which said, "God Bless Our Happy Home," sat in the corner of the sofa, and my table and two chairs sat near the window overlooking the backyard and the garage where Mrs. Plaut, from time to time, tinkered with the Model A Mr. Plaut had left to her when he died.

The day was still going fine. I took off my denim jacket, loosened my tie, and thought seriously about calling Doc Hodgdon for a game or two of handball at the YMCA. I put the groceries away in my small refrigerator and the little cupboard above it, poured myself a glass of milk, and sat down to dunk away the Hydrox cookies. If I couldn't have

Carmen for a few days, and my ex-wife Anne wouldn't talk to me on the phone, I could at least eat myself fat.

Mrs. Plaut's chapter lay before me on the table. I hadn't looked at it since she had given it to me a week before. I read the opening paragraphs:

Granny Teller first met the peddler on August the 16th in the year 1836 two days after the fact of Grandfather Teller's demise from an overindulgence in foods of a spiced nature which we now know will eat away your guts. She was need I say despondent but she had the farm to run and Ohio was remote and my mother and her brothers young. Actually Uncle Bike was not really young at that juncture, but he acted as if part of the mind was bent like a young elm branch with too many possums calling it home. Uncle Bike was oft called an Idiot, but that was unkind and possibly not even true.

To the peddler for I am sure, gentle reader, you are curious about this curious encounter. My mother told me he came on August 16 of the year given above as I have related and that his name was Lute McLain and that he wore a gray stovepipe hat which was most inappropriate for the weather in August and Ohio at any time. Granny Teller was in no mood or economic state to purchase the time of day, but Lute McLain was determined and a Baptist to boot or so he confessed. He tried pins, dry goods, crackers, even a Jews harp which much appealed to Uncle Bike but not Granny Teller.

"Well," Lute McLain said according to my mother. "I have nothing else but my son out in the wagon. He works hard, has little intellect, and is decent enough to look at." My mother looked at the wagon in front of the house and there sat a boy who looked no brighter than Bike but his nose was certainly not mashed and he had his teeth.

"No thank you," Granny Teller said according to my

mother. "I've already got one of those." She meant my Uncle Bike.

"I meant, Dear Lady, that my son Buff might make a suitable husband," said Mr. Lute McLain.

"My daughter is too young," Granny Teller said.

"But, Dear Lady, you are in your prime and have just lost your husband."

"I am fifty and one," said Granny Teller.

"Buff is eighteen," said Lute McLain. "And you can have him for twenty dollars gold."

"You have sold your son," said Granny Teller.

They were wed three weeks later when Preacher Willins from Dayton came through on his rounds. True to Lute McLain's word Buff was stupid and worked hard. Granny Teller always said he was a bargain. It was only three years later that Buff admitted that he was not the son of Lute McLain but an itinerant, a runaway who McLain had picked up in Virginia and promised to find a wife and good home.

Ten years later when Granny Teller died happy, Buff, whose name was Plaut, married my mother and later became my father. I do not remember him well since he expired in an argument with a Sioux Indian name of Sidney Worth in Kansas City when I was eleven, but my mother assured me and my sister and my brother often that our father was not nearly as dense as he had been sold to be.

There was more. I finished my cookies and milk, being careful not to get Mrs. Plaut's manuscript wet, and pulled the mattress to the floor.

I already had an idea of who might be threatening to kidnap Bette Davis and I knew where to start to check on the possibility. The potential kidnapper was Davis's first husband, and the person who could help me find out was the world's sleaziest private detective, Andrea G. Pinketts.

But first I needed a nap.

The nap was short, interrupted by Mrs. Plaut stalking into my room to announce, "The gumbatz is ready."

I don't wake up well from naps. I shouldn't nap. Unless I overdose on Pepsi and coffee, I don't come out of the fog till I've had a full night's sleep. "What?" I said, sitting up in my boxer shorts and scratching my hairy chest.

"Gumbatz," she repeated.

"I'll be right down," I said.

"Five minutes," she said, and disappeared.

I looked at my old-man's watch. Habit. It told me it was nine. The sun and the Beech-Nut clock on the wall confirmed my suspicion that my father's watch was reliably incorrect. It was four-fourteen. I got up, almost fell on my face, groped my way to my pants, and managed to dress. I staggered to the communal powder room across from my room, washed, and made it downstairs to Mrs. Plaut's door. I knocked hard and loud.

"Enter," she chirped.

Dexter wasn't where I had last seen him. Neither was his cage. I found them both in the kitchen on the table.

"Sit," ordered Mrs. Plaut.

I sat, trying to keep my eyes open. In front of me was a bowl of something brown with darker brown splotches of something in it. A spoon lay next to the bowl. I looked at Mrs. Plaut. She looked back at me and smiled, nodding her head and pointing to the bowl. I got the idea.

I took a spoonful of gumbatz, brought it to my mouth, and downed it. It tasted like nothing I had ever had before or since. Not that it was bad. It was just unfamiliar. Mrs. Plaut had no bowl in front of her.

"Very good," I said. "Aren't you having any?"

"Hate it," she said, making a face. "Men like it."

"Would you like to share a knowledge of the ingredients with me?" I asked, taking another very small spoonful of gumbatz.

"Family secret," she said.

"Do you plan to include it in your memoirs?"

"Yes, but they are to be published posthumously. That means when I'm dead."

"I know. But I'm editing your memoirs."

"You've read about Granny Teller..."

"...and Lute McLain," I finished. "Fascinating. The recipe?"

"Major ingredients only," she whispered, looking at Dexter, who was chirping away and eating the same canary food Virginia Bruce gave her bird.

I prayed that Mrs. Plaut wouldn't spell the ingredients. She didn't, but she did decide to continue whispering. "Molasses, brown sugar, flour, cumin, and possum."

"I've never eaten possum before," I said.

"I find the taste vile, but men..." She shrugged at the bad taste of the males who inhabit the earth.

"Where did you get a poss—?" I tried, but,

"My father invented gumbatz," she interrupted proudly.

"Buff Plaut, the one who was uncharitably labeled an idiot by Lute McLain," I said, wondering how to get rid of the remaining three-fifths of a bowl of gumbatz.

"I plan to take a jar to Mr. Arthur Godfrey," she said. "I'll ask Mr. Wherthman to drive me."

"May I finish this in my room?" I asked.

"Why?"

"Inspiration while I finish the chapter about your father."

I rose and took the bowl in hand while Mrs. Plaut considered my request.

"Yes," she said. "You may. But don't take too long to eat it, or get it into the refrigerator. It tends to get gamey somewhat fast.'"

"It will be gone in minutes," I assured her.

"Wait," she called, as I headed groggily back to the hallway.

"Yes, Mrs. Plaut," I said.

"Here."

She handed me something that looked like a fishing box with a thin metal handle. My left hand was full of gumbatz. I took the fishing box in my right. It was heavy.

"What is this, Mrs. Plaut?"

"Mah-Jongg," she said. "Some pieces are coming loose again, you know, tops sliding off the tiles. You are to take them to your friend with the special glue. I need them in two days when Jesse, Claire, and Eleanor come over."

I nodded. Shelly had fixed her Mah-Jongg tiles before. He said they were no different from teeth.

I went up the stairs. My first stop was the communal washroom, where the gumbatz disappeared and I washed the bowl.

My second stop was the pay telephone at the head of the stairs. I found Andrea G. Pinketts in the Los Angeles directory under *private investigators*. I fished out a nickel and called. There was an answer on the sixth ring.

"Pinketts Agency," he said. "This is Andrea Pinketts. My secretary isn't here."

"Pinketts, you don't have a secretary."

"Who is this?"

"Toby Peters."

"Toby Peters?"

"Six years ago," I reminded him. "I was just starting out as a private investigator and you hired me for a job in Coldwater Canyon."

"I remember," he said.

"Maybe I can return the favor."

"Way I remember it," said Pinketts, "you got a little upset when you found out what the job was."

"Yeah, but I did it and took the paycheck. Depression. Times were hard. I may have some work for you if you're interested."

"I'm interested," said Pinketts, who had been working into his Gilbert Roland accent as we continued to talk.

"You want me to come to your office?"

"I don't work out of an office," said Pinketts proudly. "I'm on the move too much for an office. I'll meet you somewhere."

I knew this story. I'd used it as recently as that morning.

"Fine. It's a nice day. How about—"

"There's a coffee shop, Andy's, on Melrose and Vine."

"I know it. Few blocks from Paramount."

"Right. I know the people who own it. Good people. Honest people. Coffee's on you, right?"

"Right," I said.

"I can be there in five minutes," he said. "But, my friend, the meeting is yours. You name the time."

"Twenty minutes," I said.

"Twenty minutes," he confirmed, and we both hung up.

I returned the empty bowl to Mrs. Plaut, praised her gumbatz and the memory of her father, and escaped, Mah-Jongg box in hand, in need of coffee.

It took me fifteen minutes to get to Andy's on Melrose and Vine and another three minutes to park. It's usually easy to park my battered Crosley. It fits comfortably into any space larger than a phone booth.

My one and only business deal with Andrea G. Pinketts had been a subcontract from a big agency, the kind of deal Pinketts specialized in. We put microphones in the bedroom of a house in Coldwater Canyon, a nice house. I didn't know who lived there. The big agency had been hired by the husband, a bandleader named Ham Nelson who was supposed to be working all night in a hotel in Santa Monica. The wife was out. We had plenty of time to set up. I didn't know what we were setting up for, but knowing Pinketts's reputation, I had some idea it wasn't something a top-flight agency would take on. Nelson, the husband, a nervous guy around forty with curly hair, set us up in a toolshed behind the house. Pinketts and I got the earphones and the discs ready and waited with the bandleader at our side.

Around nine a car pulled up and someone went in the house. About ten minutes later they went into the bedroom.

About two minutes after that, I knew from the voice that the woman was Bette Davis. I didn't know who the man was, but it was clear and being recorded that he had a performance problem and she was helping him.

The husband, who hung over our shoulders listening with his own earphones, waited longer than seemed reasonable for an outraged husband.

When it was clear that things were moving along with some success in the house and that the man with Bette Davis had, with her guidance, begun to perform, Nelson suddenly said, "Turn it off. Stop recording. Leave the record here and go. Now. You'll have my check in the morning."

"Right," Pinketts had said, hitting a switch and taking off his earphones.

Nelson dashed out of the shed and Pinketts put his earphones back on. He put in a fresh disc and started a new recording.

"Pinketts," I had said, "the man told us to—"

"You want to get paid," he said. "Shut up."

I shut up and listened.

Ham Nelson stormed through the house and burst into the bedroom. About ten seconds later, Pinketts and I knew that the guy in the bedroom with the problem was Howard Hughes. Twenty seconds beyond that we learned that Ham Nelson wanted fifty thousand dollars cash to turn the record over to Hughes. Hughes immediately agreed, and Nelson promised to hand him the record in the morning when Hughes gave him the cash.

That's when Pinketts had said, "Let's go."

He stopped the machine, took out the disc he had just recorded, the one with Ham Nelson blackmailing Davis and Hughes, and shoved it in his briefcase. He left the first record, the one Nelson had told us to leave, on the table. Then we left.

In a bar three blocks away Pinketts paid me in cash, lit

one of his trademark thin cigars, and sauntered into the night.

I hadn't heard from Pinketts again.

I did read in *Variety* that Davis and Nelson had been divorced a little later.

When I'd worked at Warners a few years earlier, I had run into Bette Davis more than a few times. We had exchanged nods, words, maybe a "good morning" or "good night," no more than she did with any other uniformed studio guard, but she had been friendly enough.

The word on the lot had been that she was a decent sort, feet on the ground, who got a bad deal from the Brothers Warner. She'd tried to break her contract, get more money, do less than three or four pictures a year, and get some say-so in picking them. She'd gone to court in England and lost. Though the trades wondered what she was complaining about, the people who worked on the lot knew that she was getting paid far less than any of the male leads, including Cagney, Flynn, Raft, Bogart, or even Edward G. Robinson, all of whom had the right to turn down projects. And this was after she had won an Oscar and was reported to be one of the top three box-office draws in the world.

The money Pinketts had paid me went into one of Shelly Minck's schemes, pastel-colored false teeth. He had assured me that it was more than a fad, that pink teeth were going over big on the Riviera. I lost every cent and I was glad I did.

Now that record was back to haunt me.

Andy's wasn't anything special, but I'm not exactly the gourmet editor of the *L.A. Times*. It was a mid-block coffee house for below-the-line assistants at Paramount. Grips, gaffers, gofers, and extras hung around places like Andy's making contacts, killing time, making it clear where they could be found. But there was no crowd that Monday when I stepped in, and even if there had been, the place was small and Pinketts easy to spot.

He hadn't changed.

He was about five-ten or -eleven, lean, dark, with a full head of black curly hair, an aura of perpetual weariness, and that omnipresent thin cigar in his mouth or hand. He wore dark suits and liked to drape a scarf around his neck. Few had seen his dark eyes behind the sunglasses he seldom removed. People who passed him on the street or saw him walking down Sunset or Hollywood would ask him for his autograph, which he always graciously gave. The people then went home to decipher the scrawl and figure out who this movie star might be. Most of them guessed he was Gilbert Roland or Cesar Romero, and that was close enough for Pinketts, whose parents had both been Rumanian farmers.

"Toby," he said from a booth in the rear, lifting a weary arm in greeting. "It is so good to see you again, my old friend."

"Andrea," I said, moving toward him.

The guy behind the counter was fat, in his fifties, and unimpressed by either of us.

I shook Pinketts's hand and sat across from him in the booth.

"Coffee?" he asked.

"A gallon," I said.

Pinketts waved at the fat guy behind the counter.

"Coffees," Pinketts called. "And I'm a bit hungry. Let us try the fried-chicken special, a double coleslaw, mashed potatoes, and your homemade apple pie."

"Not for me," I said. "Just coffee."

Up close, Pinketts was definitely six years older and at least six years shabbier. The scarf around his neck was just about out of life and color, and I had the feeling it was draped carefully to cover some rough spots in the jacket.

"You look much the same, my old partner in arms," he said.

"I look older," I said. "I cut the sideburns so the gray shows a little less and I check the mirror every morning to see if

I still look tough or look like a bum trying to look tough."

"In this business," Pinketts said, welcoming the cups of coffee placed in front of us by the fat counterman, "we gamble, amigo. Our appearance, our reputation. We are mariners in a sea of troubled lives."

The fat guy walked away.

"That Andy?" I asked.

"There is no Andy," said Pinketts. "Andy is Andy Gump, the cartoon character. Paramount once considered a series, live, not animated. Lots of publicity. A woman who later went back to Houston, Texas, had a cartoon of Andy Gump painted on a sign and hung over this shop. A few tourists came, but the bread-and-butter workers at Paramount stayed away until the sign came down."

"A Hollywood story," I said, downing most of my first cup of coffee and hoping it would bring me back to the land of the living.

"A Hollywood story," he said. "One of the sad, the comic thousands of stories. Now, I have told you a story and you have bought my attention with the price of a meal. Business."

I hadn't promised Pinketts a meal, but I nodded. "The record," I said.

"Record?"

"The one we did of Ham Nelson blackmailing Howard Hughes and Bette Davis," I reminded him.

Pinketts leaned forward to look at me over the tops of his dark glasses.

"History," he said. "You were paid."

"I'm not after more money. I want to know what you did with it."

"I sold it for far, far too little to a dealer. I might as well tell you, since I cannot share with you what I have long since spent. I got ten thousand dollars. Invested it in an office and a starlet wife, a golden creature of Amazonian proportions and beauty. It was amazing how quickly both she and the money vanished."

"I spent my two hundred dollars on pink teeth. Who did you sell it to?" I asked.

Pinketts removed the thin cigar from his mouth, drank some coffee, and regarded me for a full minute.

"What will I earn for giving you this valuable information?"

"Four thousand nine hundred and eighty dollars. My share of the sale of that recording minus the two hundred."

"Ah, but that is all money in the past. An additional five hundred dollars in the present..."

"One hundred dollars and maybe some night work at twenty a day for keeping an eye on Bette Davis."

Pinketts thought about the offer for two whole seconds.

"Cash?"

"The hundred right here and now," I said, reaching for my wallet.

He held out his hand and I counted out five twenties.

"Grover Niles," he said.

"Grover Ni... The agent?"

"The agent," said Pinketts. "He paid in cash for the record, and I walked away and did not look back."

"Did you tell Niles I knew about the recording?" I asked.

"What possible reason would I?..."

"You told him," I said.

"I told him," Pinketts agreed, tilting his head back to blow smoke at the ceiling. "But that was long ago, another life. What difference does it make now?"

"Someone who knows I was with you on that job wants to sell the record to Bette Davis's husband," I explained. "And he wants me to middleman."

"Most interesting," said Pinketts, studying me for guile.

I had three more coffees and a Pepsi. Pinketts watched me and told a series of stories as he ate his Andy's special. He had gory stories of the stars and the starstruck and he had an appetite. When he finally finished, I paid the bill and told him I'd be in touch with him.

He burped discreetly and waved regally, saying, "Be as cautious as the wind and silent as the night, amigo."

"I'll try, Pinketts," I said, and I left Andy's, not bothering to figure out what the hell if anything he might mean.

For a hundred dollars of Arthur Farnsworth's money I had bought a name. I knew Grover Niles.

No great surprise. Los Angeles is big, but the people in it holding onto the sharp edges of the movie business—the would-be's, watchers, wise guys, bamboozlers, babes, bozos, agents, flatfeet, and used-to-be's—all know each other.

How did I know Niles?

In the spring of '38 a client of mine, a whistler and birdcaller with a traveling burlesque show, claimed Niles owed her two months' pay. Niles had gotten the client, Rose-Rose Shale, two weeks in the Red Hot Blues Club on Ventura. Rose-Rose really wanted to break into movies, and Niles promised her rockets to the moon.

Rose-Rose looked great in spangles and she really could whistle like Jolson, but she had the brain of a wren, one of the few birds she did not mimic. Moe Burnhoff, the punch-drunk ex-middleweight who gave out towels at the Adriatic Gym, could have told Rose-Rose that there was no future in the movies for a whistler.

But Niles told her she had beauty, talent, and enough money saved to carry her through till Grover Niles pushed her into the path of onrushing destiny. Niles did not tell her that the Red Hot Blues Club expected something more than birdcalls for their seventy-five bucks a week. They expected her to shed some feathers.

Rose-Rose had a good heart and I took her case on for a little more than birdseed.

Niles denied owing her the money, claimed she owed him his ten percent. Grover Niles was a hard man to believe. Short, thin, with a pockmarked face and sweaty hands, Niles looked and acted nervous and carried a wrinkled handkerchief to wipe his face. Niles was no more than forty but he looked sixty, and if ever a man looked guilty of everything, it was Grover Niles.

We came to a compromise, did Grover Niles and me. He paid Rose-Rose a week's wages and got her out of the second week of her contract at the Red Hot Blues Club, and I, in return, agreed not to satisfy my curiosity by looking into his past—when, according to Rose-Rose, his name had been Wesley Sternham and he had lived in Ypsilanti, Michigan, with his wife, two kids, and a large number of markers held by the Purple Gang in Detroit.

I had not seen Niles since that episode, but I had heard his name from time to time, usually spoken with a disclaimer.

According to both the phone book and my memory, Niles's office was on Sunset near Highland. Good address but a decaying office, perched over a bakery that specialized in movie-star cookies and cakes. I parked my Crosley about a half block away near a hotel undergoing renovations and locked the doors. I had a .38 in the glove compartment and Mrs. Plaut's Mah-Jongg case in the back seat. I was more worried about losing the Mah-Jongg case.

The Crosley had been given a twice-over by No-Neck Arnie, the mechanic near my office. Since I had bought the car from him in the first place, he had recently given me a special deal to fix the broken window, the ax hole in the hood, and the driver-side door that wouldn't open. He'd also repainted the car a very off green. It looked a little like a kidney stone my old man passed on his forty-first birthday, but it ran.

A maybe-rain was in the air. I was in a good mood and a thin blue zipper jacket. It had been raining a lot this winter and I needed some new clothes, or some clean ones. I ducked into the bakery a step before the storm hit. Today's specials were chocolate Willie Bests, gingerbread W. C. Fieldses, and vanilla Shirley Temples. I bought a dozen Fieldses and Temples from the smiling old lady behind the counter and munched on Curly Top while I waited for the storm to pass.

"Ran out of FDRs early," the old lady said while I watched people dash through puddles outside. "His birthday was Saturday."

I was through all of the vanilla curls and was down to the beaming smile. I bit into it. I smiled back at the proprietress.

"We try to keep up with famous birthdays," she said.

"Doesn't the agent . . . what's his name, Niles, Grover Niles, have his office upstairs?"

The old lady wiped her hands on her white apron at the sound of Niles's name.

"Yes," she said, busying herself with cookie trays.

"Which ones are the hardest?" I asked.

"Which—?"

"Stars are the hardest?" I explained, starting on a W.C.

"Oh." She paused, tray in hand, and looked out the window at the rain for inspiration. "Leading men, women," she said. "Hard to tell a Tyrone Power from a Robert Taylor, or an Ann Sheridan from a Mary Astor in a cookie or even a cake. Comedians and kids are easy. Tell you a secret."

I looked serious and tried to keep the ginger crumbs in my mouth.

"You know who this is?"

She was holding up a Willie Best.

"Willie Best," I said.

"To you, Willie Best. I sold two dozen to Lew Ayres. Thought he was buying Stepin Fetchit."

"Why not say it's Bill Robinson and pair him up with Shirley Temple?" I suggested.

The idea struck home; she beamed at me and decided to give me a crumb of information as she rearranged a tray of Lassies a young boy brought in from the rear of the shop.

"He owe you much?" the woman asked.

"Who?" I said, walking over to catch the kitchen smells and observe better her arrangement of the kennel.

"Niles," she said. "You process server, collection agency?"

"Private detective," I said, shifting my bag of cookies so I could pull out my wallet and show it to her. "Toby Peters."

"Howard Duff on the radio is one of my favorites," she said. "Saw a picture of him in a fan magazine. I could do a Howard Duff cookie."

"Call it a Sam Spade cookie," I suggested, putting my wallet away. "Nobody knows what Duff looks like."

"Then the customers would think it was a bad Bogart."

"Niles," I reminded her.

"Deadbeat," she said pleasantly. "Always behind in rent. Landlord's going to toss him next month for sure."

The kind of guy who might pull out his nest egg, a record he bought in 1938.

"Busted," she said. "I ought to know. I own the building. What'd he do now?"

"It isn't now. It was five, six years ago. He up there?"

"Yeah," she said, backing away from the display case to survey her dog cookies upside down. "Heard him walking around."

"Rain's slowing a little," I said.

"A little. Dogs are easy," she said, rearranging the cookies a little more. "Asta's a favorite. No one knows Rin-Tin-Tin anymore."

I moved to the door.

"Come back when we've got Laurel and Hardy. Usually Thursdays. Big sellers. Easy to do."

"Thanks," I said and ducked through a few feet of light rain to the entrance to GROVER NILES, THEATRICAL BOOKINGS, UPSTAIRS.

I opened the door and made my way up the stairs. They were narrow, but reasonably well lighted and clean. I gave credit for that, right or wrong, to the cookie-baking landlady.

Niles's door was just where I'd left it five years before. The years had not been kind to her. She was losing paint. I walked in. The waiting room had changed. There were still five wooden chairs along the wall for the deluge of clients, and a reception desk facing the door. The room was just as empty as it had been the last time I had been here.

Grover Niles had neither receptionist nor secretary, and clients had always been scarce. What Niles did have was photographs on the wall, each inscribed. I looked at a few of them. It didn't evade the keen eye of Toby Peters that the signature of Marlene Dietrich under the words, "With gratitude to the jewel of all the Niles," and the signature of Richard Barthlemess under the inscription, "I don't know where I'd have been without you, Grover," were suspiciously similar.

"You need help?" came a quivering man's voice behind me.

I turned slowly to face Niles, who looked pretty much the same as he had in '38, if you overlooked the fact that he was ten times as nervous. He had added one thing, a pair of suspenders.

"Remember me?" I asked with a smile, stepping toward him.

The look on his twitching face was close to panic as he backed away.

"Hey, I told him I was deaf and dumb," Niles said, wiping his face with the handkerchief in his right hand and holding out his left in the hope that the gesture would keep me from advancing.

"You told him?"

"I'm safe," he whimpered. "I'm zipped tight."

"Have a cookie," I said, holding out the bag. "I recommend the Shirley Temples."

Grover Niles didn't want a cookie.

"The old lady downstairs has great ears," he said, his back against the wall as I put my hand into the cookie bag. "She'll hear."

"She'll hear me give you a cookie?"

"You're toyin' with me." He almost wept. "Christ, don't toy with me. You're gonna shoot me, stab me, something."

"Who you afraid of, Grover?" I asked, pulling out a Shirley Temple and a W. C. Fields and holding them out to him. "Take 'em."

He took a cookie.

"I'm not supposed to eat sweets," he said, putting the Fields to his mouth without looking at it. "Doctor says I'm a borderline diabetic, you know. This isn't, you know, I mean these aren't my last cookies? They're not...you didn't put something in 'em?"

"Rose-Rose Shale," I said. "Remember?"

He dropped his cookie.

"Rose-Rose?"

"Thirty-eight. You stiffed her for seventy-five bucks. I came for it. I don't know what happened to Rose-Rose, but I know what happened to you. You turned into a lump of cranberry sauce."

"You...you're the shamus," he said with sudden relief, moving to the receptionist's chair and plopping down.

"You remember Rose-Rose?" I asked.

"Remember her? I married her," said Grover Niles, letting out a deep breath of air. "Two great months. Then she left me. Only time I ever married, if you don't count Yolanda."

"Let's not count Yolanda. Let's talk business. A little after you met your future bride you bought a record from a man named Pinketts for ten thousand dollars."

"I knew it," screamed Niles, leaping to his feet. "Wiklund."

"Who's Wiklund? The guy you sold the record to?"

"I don't know about any records. I don't remember any records. Wiklund is an actor—lousy, two bit. Name just popped out. You know the way it is. I've been under a lot of strain since the war."

"You paid ten thousand for the record. Bette Davis, Howard

Hughes, and Ham Nelson in 'Goodnight, Ladies.' Grover, don't tell me you forgot a ten-thousand-dollar deal."

"My memory is bad," he said, looking at the door behind me. "It's the diabetes. I'm a sick man. I've never been a ten-thousand-dollar dealer."

"Then you fronted for someone," I tried. "I've got a guess. It's wild and if I get it wrong, I want two more chances. Was his name Wiklund?"

Grover Niles lurched as if he had been given a jolt of electricity.

"Oh, Jesus," he groaned, wiping his forehead and neck. "Oh, Jesus, Jesus, Jesus."

"No, I don't think his name was Jesus. Let me make another guess. Pinketts told you I worked on that job bugging Bette Davis and Howard Hughes. You told Wiklund. And just before I came through that door, somebody, Pinketts maybe, called you and told you to get out."

"No," said Niles, fanning his arms in front of him. "No. No."

"Maybe you should have stuck to bird whistlers, dialect comics, and accordion players, Grover," I said. "You don't lie well enough for this business."

"I used to," he said, shaking his head. "I used to lie with the best of 'em, the very best. Maybe we can make a deal here. Your brother's the cop, what's his name? . . ."

"Phil Pevsner, the Wilshire. How do you know?"

"How do I . . . I stay alive knowing things like that. Let's deal here. You get me to your brother. I talk to him, tell him. Then you give me enough to get on a train for Cincy or even a bus to Reno. I got friends . . . well, maybe not friends, but people I know in Cincy, Reno."

"Let's just talk a while here," I said.

"Let's just talk someplace else," he said, coming around the desk and trying to get past me. I grabbed his arm. I may have been musty from the rain, but Grover was wet with sweat and definitely ripe.

"We got to get out of here. First, Pinketts tells me to stay here, that he'll be right over with a deal. Then you show up. You tell me he sent you. I figure he sold me out to you. He could sell me out to them."

"Them?"

"The guys I middled for on the record."

"Wiklund?"

"Yeah. Jesus. I thought this was old history and now it's back. What's going on? Wait, who cares? These guys are not good guys, Peters. Let's get the hell out of here. Pinketts is setting us both up."

Niles tried to pull away.

"You've got an active imagination."

"I've got no goddamn imagination at all," he bleated. "That's why I'm broke and tryin' to mooch a bus ticket to Cincy or Reno. Humor me."

"Okay," I said, letting him go. "Let's find someplace else to talk."

He hurried past me and opened the door. I tucked the cookie bag in the pocket of my zip-up and followed him.

The first shot came when he stepped onto the landing outside the door. The second shot came when I stepped back from the door and watched Grover Niles turn toward me as his knees gave way. His handkerchief was in his hand and he was reaching up to mop his brow.

The second shot took him somewhere on the right side. He spun toward it and disappeared down the stairwell. I heard his body clumping.

There was no point in wishing I had taken my .38 out of the glove compartment. There had been no reason to think I might need it. It hadn't done me much good the few times I had called on it in the past. In the best of situations I was a lousy shot, but a few bullets fired in a situation like this might make a killer pause instead of rushing up a stairway like Dillinger.

I listened, back against the wall. He didn't rush up the stairs.

He would probably just turn around and run. No self-respecting killer would jump over a victim and go up a flight of stairs to a possible dead end when a beat cop who heard some shots might be right behind him.

I was wrong. This was a highly motivated killer who didn't want to leave any witnesses. I could hear his footsteps coming up the stairs: steady, light, and even. I grabbed the biggest framed photograph on the wall, Claudette Colbert. She was smiling sweetly and looking over her right shoulder.

The footsteps were almost at the top of the stairs. The door was open slightly. I stuck my left foot out, eased the door open with it, and stepped onto the landing, swinging Claudette with two hands. If he was a step too low I'd hit air and take a bullet.

The picture hit him dead solid on the side of his head. He got off one shot that went up somewhere as he tumbled backward. I started after him and watched him lose his gun and sprawl over the body of Grover Niles, who hadn't quite made it to the bottom.

He came up with a bloody face and a dazed look. The gun was on a step midway between us. The difference was he'd have to scramble over the late Grover Niles to get to it first. I didn't get a good look at him, but it was enough. I was sure I'd recognize him again if I saw him, especially if I saw him in the next few weeks before his face healed.

I went for the gun and he went for the door.

When I came up with the gun and took ten steps down, a figure appeared in the doorway below. I came close to shooting the cop, but he came just as close to shooting me.

"Put it down easy, you son of a bitch," he called.

I bent my knees and put the gun on the steps.

"A guy just ran out of here with..."

"Hands in the air and down the stairs slow," he said.

He sounded scared. Not as scared as Grover Niles had

sounded, apparently with good reason, but scared. I put my hands up and moved down slowly.

I stepped around Niles's body, which was no easy trick on the narrow stairway, and said gently, "You know what I'm going to say?"

"You didn't do it," he guessed.

I guessed the cop's age at twelve, but I didn't tell him. He had the gun and I had the problem.

"Right."

He backed away, gun leveled at my stomach. We went out into the street and found a small crowd waiting in the drizzle. The crowd included the old lady from the bakery.

"First homicide?" I said softly to the young cop.

"Yes," he said, wondering what to do next. It wasn't that tough, but when you suddenly find a corpse and a homely man with a gun in his hand, your memory sometimes goes for a walk.

"Ask one of the bystanders to call for backup," I suggested. "Wilshire's not far. I suggest they ask for Captain Pevsner or Lieutenant Seidman."

The young cop looked bewildered.

"I'll call," said the bakery lady. "Pevsner and Seidman."

"Right," I said.

The rain started again and the crowd reluctantly moved on. The cop and I were alone, and the cookies in my pocket were getting soggy.

"How about we go inside the bakery?" I suggested.

"We stay here," he said, blinking his eyes. "We stay right here till I get backup."

And that's what we did. We stood in the drizzle till Steven Seidman pulled up in an unmarked Ford coupe, looked at the cop and then at me, and shook his head.

Ten minutes later, after Seidman had looked at Niles's corpse, heard the young cop's tale and told him to write a 243 Report, Seidman pointed me toward the Ford. I got in and we drove off, leaving the young cop bewildered in the rain.

Five minutes later he stopped in front of the Peppy Pup hot-dog stand, which was shaped like a big dog. We got out and walked over to the outdoor table.

My brother Phil was eating a Peppy Pup hot-dog sandwich. He waved the tail end at a second one on a plate in front of him. Fries surrounded it. I wasn't hungry, but there was an outside chance, far outside, that this was a kind of peace offering, a gesture of good will from my brother the cop. At least that's what I wanted to think.

"Yeah, thanks," I said and reached for the dog.

Phil was sitting at the metal table painted white in front of the Peppy Pup. I sat across from him. An umbrella was over us, but we didn't need it at the moment. The rain had stopped. Steve Seidman, my brother's partner for the past two decades, stood behind Phil, pale, bored, his arms folded, his hat tilted back to show his high forehead.

I took a bite of the sandwich and looked out at the traffic on Melrose swishing by. The mustard, onions, and relish were fine, but it needed texture. I started to stuff fries into what remained of the dog.

"Don't do that," Phil said, a wad of sandwich in his cheek.

I stopped stuffing fries and ate.

My brother is five years older than I am, forty pounds heavier, and much less friendly. He looks something like a big standing steamer trunk. His short hair is gray. His tie is usually loose and his collar open. He always looks as if he ate a few seconds ago and it didn't agree with him.

Phil had two passions. First, he hated criminals, believed it was his mission, his duty, to destroy them all without a trial. His dedication had earned him a wartime promotion as a district captain. His nearly religious fury had booted him back to Wilshire. Phil's second passion was his family: his suffering, smiling stick of a wife, Ruth, with her mop of straw-yellow hair, and his three kids, Dave, Nate, and Lucy.

Sometimes I was included. Usually not. I owed my smashed nose to Phil. He wasn't the only one who had broken it, but he held the record, twice. I think he wanted me to make something of my life, be a violinist or sell muddy lots in Sherman Oaks. I was a great disappointment to him the day I was born, which happened to be the same day our mother died.

Phil finished his sandwich and watched me finish mine and play with the fries. I was in no hurry. I looked at the Peppy Pup behind Seidman and my brother. The pup was big and happy in spite of the chips of paint that had been taken from him by wind, heat, and rain. From the hole in his belly a guy with a worry was doling out hot dogs and Green Rivers.

"Finished?" asked Phil.

I looked up at him and then at Seidman.

"Finished," I said, wiping my mouth with a napkin. "What are we doing here?"

"Having dinner, conducting business," said Phil, resting his big hands on the table. "Wilshire's being painted."

"Your allergies," I said.

"It'll take two, maybe three days before I can go back in. Steve and I have been moving around."

I nodded in understanding. Phil had suffered from allergies all his life. His favorite was fresh paint, which closed his sinuses and made him itch. Next came strawberries, which made his hands swell, and finally came fresh coconut, which made him throw up.

"Sorry," I said. "How are? . . ."

"Don't," Phil said with a warning smile, holding up his right hand.

"Don't, Toby," Seidman added.

I had been about to say, "How are Ruth and the kids?" a question that sent my brother into a rage. I'm not sure why. I don't think he is, either, but it's a fact that has to be honored except when I'm feeling lucky or there's a mischief in me. I wasn't feeling either.

"Toby," Phil said, pushing the empty plates out of the way and leaning toward me. "Ruth's surgery had some problems. It's taking her a little longer to recover than the asshole of a doctor promised us. Now, with your cooperation here there is a chance I might be able to get home tonight before the kids get to sleep. You gonna help me?"

"Absolutely," I said amiably.

"Good," said Phil. "Tell us what happened. Whole thing. No lies. No bullshit about protecting clients. Tell it fast. Tell it convincing. And then we decide what to do."

"Give me a second to think about this," I said.

"No," Phil answered with a pained, knowing smile. "You don't understand, Tobias. It was not a request. Talk or suffer."

"You're going to beat your own brother on a public street in front of a giant puppy?"

"I've done things which have shown even less control," said Phil. "You've seen some of them. Steve has seen a few more."

"I've seen more than I want to see, Phil," Seidman said.

"Started around lunchtime today," I said. "Client."

"Name of client?" said Phil softly, as Seidman took notes.

"Arthur."

"Arthur? That a first or last name?"

"I don't know. That's all he gave me, that and a cash advance."

Phil's chunky fingers began to play with the edge of the plate. "Go on."

"Well," I said, "he said someone was trying to blackmail him about a recording made of his wife and another guy." Phil was shaking his head in disbelief. I kept on talking. "I found out from a guy that..."

"A guy?" asked Phil. "Guy have a name, a first and last name?"

"He's not important. He's just a guy who knew who had the record," I said impatiently.

"Record of your client's wife and another guy," Phil supplied.

"Right," I said admiringly, as if he'd just won a box of Milky Ways on "Dr. I.Q."

"Wife and the other guy have a name?"

"Everybody's got a name, Phil," I whined. "I don't know theirs."

"Go on," he said.

I didn't like the way his hands were clenching and unclenching. "Well, the guy gives me the name of Grover Niles, says Niles has the record or knows who does. I go to Niles, ask him. He says he knows who has the record—who must be trying to blackmail my client. Niles was about to take me to the blackmailer when he got shot. Killer came up after me. I hit him with a picture. You'll find it up there. He went down the stairs, dropped the gun he shot Niles with. I picked up the gun and he ran."

"You get a good look at the killer?"

"Good enough," I said, sitting back.

"That's it?" asked Phil.

"I've got nothing else, Phil, except a pocketful of cookie pieces and crumbs." I tried to look like a cherub. I grinned, shrugged, held out my hands, palms up. If my brother was going to destroy me, the time was now.

"I believe you," he said. "Except for the shit about not knowing anybody's name. Steve?"

"As far as it goes," added Seidman, putting away his notebook.

"As far as it goes," agreed Phil. "You figure the blackmailer found you, knew Grover would talk, and shot him?"

"Something like that," I agreed. "Makes sense."

"How'd he know you were with Niles?"

"I don't know," I said, shaking my head. "I wish I had some idea."

Phil got up. I started to do the same. He motioned for me

to sit down and moved to my side, leaning down to whisper in my ear. His right hand touched my shoulder. His fingers dug in deep. I kept looking at the belly of the pup beyond Seidman.

"Talk to your client," he whispered. "Tell him the police want his name, the police want to talk to him about blackmail and murder. Tomorrow you call, give me your client's name and address, and tell him to come see me. You understand?"

"I understand, Phil."

His fingers came out of my shoulder, leaving an indented jacket and bruised flesh.

"Good. You want to come over for dinner, maybe Sunday, if Ruth's up to it? Ruth and the kids ask about you."

"Sure," I said.

"Ruth's making stuffed cabbage," he explained. "Come anytime in the afternoon."

"Okay. I've had a busy day and I'd better track down my client."

Phil didn't say anything. He moved slowly toward the curb where Seidman's car was parked.

"Have your client call tomorrow," Seidman reminded me, adjusting his hat. "Walk easy, Toby."

"You forgot to say Seidman says," I said.

"Never heard that one before," Seidman said deadpan, as he turned and took a step toward his car.

"Hey," I called after them. "What about my car? I left it parked near Niles's office."

I think Phil shrugged. No one answered. I sat there and watched them get into the car and drive away.

Chapter Four

I had cash and Arthur Farnsworth was paying and, so far, getting his money's worth. I hailed a Black and White cab and had him drive me back to my Crosley, which had a ticket under the windshield wiper. I pulled into evening traffic, turned on the radio, and searched. I heard Walter Huston's voice first, then Bette Davis's rasping answer. I didn't know *Dodsworth*, but I figured out fast that Davis was playing Dodsworth's wife, that she had been fooling around, and that he wasn't happy about it. It sounded too much like real life. I turned it off and headed for the radio station.

I got there just as the broadcast was ending. I already had one parking ticket in the glove compartment, next to my .38. I had to risk another one. I pulled into a parking lot marked Staff Only, looking for a guard to talk my way past. No one appeared. I found a space next to a big DeSoto, got out, and went in search of Bette Davis.

People were streaming out of the building, probably the audience for *Dodsworth*. I moved with a small chattering crowd of women, young girls, and a few men, two of them sailors, to the side of the building. It was dark but I felt the winter threat of returning rain. A few of the women gave up after five minutes. A few others held out with me.

"Where's your book?" asked the guy at my side, all teeth and smiles and far from young.

"Book?"

"Autograph book," he said, holding up his book to show me. "I don't have Walter Huston," he explained. "I could always use another Bette, anyone could."

"I agree," I said.

"Here they come," said a woman in the front of the group.

The door, up two concrete steps, opened. Two men and a couple of women stepped out, ignored the crowd, and kept walking. Then Huston appeared. He grinned broadly, acted surprised at the gathering, and moved down to sign autographs. The guy at my side lumbered toward him with his book open and his Parker pen at the ready.

Bette Davis came out a few steps behind Huston and the crowd split. About ten people, including the sailors, surrounded her. She smiled gently, exchanged a few words as she signed.

Davis was wearing a gray dress with a silver necklace. Over the dress she wore a matching cape, its hood covering her head and shading her eyes.

Autograph seekers moved from her to Huston as a few were doing the reverse. Huston finished first, waved at Davis who blew him a kiss, and moved briskly into the parking lot as the guy I had been talking to tried to follow him.

"Sorry," said Huston, turning back. "Another appointment."

The guy stopped and hurried back toward Davis, who was just finishing the last woman and now turned her attention to the sailors. She was interrupted by Autograph Harry, politely signed, and continued talking to the sailors as Harry waddled away with his prize.

I was about six feet away when she looked up at me.

Recognition took a few seconds. She turned back to the sailors.

"And what are you two planning for the rest of the evening?" she asked.

Neither boy knew what to say.

"Movie, maybe a beer, and back to the hotel."

"Shipping out tomorrow," the second one said.

"I have an idea," Davis said. "I'm on my way to the Hollywood Canteen. Are you familiar with it?"

"I think . . . I don't know, Cal?"

"I don't think so," said Cal. "Maybe I think I've heard of it."

"You have a car?" she asked.

"No," said Cal.

"Good," she said, taking their arms. "Come with me. I'll drive."

Both kids were beaming as they moved into the lot, locked to Bette Davis. They gave me wait-till-we-tell-the-guys-on-the-ship grins as they moved past me. Davis slowed half a beat and looked at me again, trying to place me, maybe wondering what I was doing there, and then she moved on.

I gave them time to get to her car and drive off. I didn't have to tail them. I knew where the Hollywood Canteen was.

Fifteen minutes later I was driving down Sunset, worrying about all the gas I was using and how few gas ration stamps I had left.

The location of the Hollywood Canteen, about a block off of Sunset, was fine unless you wanted to park a car. According to Shelly Minck, the myopic dentist, the Canteen had been started the year before by Davis. John Garfield, who was 4F and feeling guilty about it, had come to Davis while she was making *Now, Voyager* and suggested that she head a drive of movie people to run a place where soldiers and sailors about to ship out to the Pacific or just coming in for leave could meet stars like Davis, Dietrich, and Grable, dance with starlets, and be entertained by acts like Bob Hope and the Mills Brothers.

The place, an old theater and dance hall, was refurbished by movie-studio craftsmen donating their time and movie studios donating paint and parts. Business boomed from the start. Supposedly two thousand movie people did shifts serving, dancing, entertaining, and even cleaning up, and every night more than a thousand kids in uniform came through the doors.

The only uniform I had was a spare night-watchman's brown slacks, jacket, and cap I had to buy when I pulled down regular nights for two weeks in the parking lot of the Brown Derby the year before.

I parked about a block from the Canteen in a spot big enough for a straight-up quarter or a Crosley. I could hear the music when I stepped out of the car.

A guy in a flannel shirt was sitting on the steps of a house next to the place where I parked. He was about sixty, burly, with gray curly hair, reminded me of Alan Hale.

"Visiting somebody?" he asked.

"Yeah," I said, locking the driver's side door and turning to him.

The man was shaking his head.

"Hear that?"

The music from the Hollywood Canteen was loud, full of brass and saxophone.

"I hear it," I said.

"Every night," he said. "Most of the night. I'm on the early shift at Lockheed all the way out in Burbank. Some shift I'm gonna get my hand pulped. I get no sleep."

"Shame," I said, taking a step toward him.

"Well," he said, and sighed. "You know. What can you do? The war. Some of those kids, a lot of 'em, they won't be coming... hell, I've got a kid in the Pacific somewhere, marine. I'll live with it."

"How long have you lived here?" I asked.

"Twenty-eight years," he said, looking over his shoulder at the house. "I'll probably die here."

There was a trombone blast from the direction of the canteen, followed by roars, applause, and whistling. A new song blared up almost immediately.

"Know much about the Canteen?" I asked.

"Much? Like what?"

"Anybody get in there besides guys in uniform?"

"Girls in uniform get in," he said.

"And?..."

"People who work there. Movie people. Know why I'm sitting out here?"

"Can't sleep," I guessed.

"Naw. I get to see movie stars. When the Canteen lot gets filled they park down here. Almost every night I see someone, write to Hal about it. Hal's my son. See Bette Davis a lot. That *Prisoner of Zenda* guy... Ronald Colman. Saw him yesterday. Hal likes movies. Gene Tierney's his favorite. You figurin' on crashin' the door?"

"Looking for someone who might be in there," I said. "Civilian."

"Good luck," he said over a tenor sax solo, and I moved back to my Crosley, opened the door, reached into the back seat, pulled out the carrying case with Mrs. Plaut's Mah-Jongg box inside, and headed down the street toward the blasting trumpets and hooting voices. A quartet of marines moved toward the door in front of me. I zipped my jacket up, tucked the Mah-Jongg box under my arm, and started through the door.

"Servicemen and women only," a voice said, as an arm was shoved in front of me.

I shifted the Mah-Jongg box with a grunt, reached into my pocket, and fished out my wallet.

"Peters, Warner grip," I said, finding my long-expired ID card as uniformed kids moved past me to the not-quite-hot trumpet of Harry James, soloing on "Cherry." Give me Muggsy Spanier any day. "How do I get to the light grids? Miss Davis called, asked me to stop by on the way home. Short or something."

I didn't recognize the guys at the door. They weren't kids but they weren't lightweights either. I figured them for security staff from Columbia or Republic. They lacked the refinement of the older studios.

The guy who had his arm out glanced at the ID card, saw the Warner shield and my name.

"Al, you know where the grid is?"

Al was busy ushering people through the door.

"Nah."

"That's okay," I said. "I'll find it."

The arm came down and I walked into the Canteen. There was a small lobby, beyond which the doors leading inside were open. A fog of cigarette smoke filled the space. About a dozen servicemen and starlets were smoking, talking, smiling.

I walked inside and looked up at the low stage. Harry James and his orchestra were behind a low chain, bleating the melancholy tune while couples danced beneath light fixtures that looked like kerosene lamps. The lights had been turned low.

At first I didn't see Bette Davis. I saw Olivia De Havilland talking to a pair of soldiers in a corner, and Ginger Rogers cheek to cheek on the dance floor with a sailor who looked like my twelve-year-old nephew, Nate, but no Davis.

I hefted my Mah-Jongg toolbox and pushed my way through the crowd, with apologies. I wasn't the only man in civvies in the place, but the others were either on the bandstand, serving food, or looking like movie stars I should recognize, in perfectly pressed suits.

"I'm here," came a familiar voice.

I turned, almost hit a kid in an air-force uniform with my box, and found myself looking at Bette Davis no more than half a dozen feet in front of me. She strode forward around two couples and stood in front of me with a smile that could kill. The orchestra had picked up the theme and it was hard to hear her as she said, "Why are you following me?"

"I'm not following you," I said, surprised. "I'm an electrician. I was over at NBC when I got a call that the lights—"

"Your name is Peters," she said. "You used to be a guard at Warner Brothers. Now, you have either become an electrician who, for some reason which I cannot conceive, has decided to carry his tools in a Mah-Jongg case, or you are lying."

"You remember me," I said. "It was more than—"

"As I recall," she interrupted, "we had a similar distaste for the behavior of Jack Warner."

"He fired me," I said.

"I know. Ironically, Mr. Warner has been remarkably generous in providing craftsmen and even dollars to the Canteen. Why are you following me, Mr. Peters?"

The music rose and I asked Davis, "Someplace we can talk?"

She turned without a word, and I followed her to a door in the far wall, away from the entrance. She pushed it open and I followed her in. The closed door cut out most of the sounds from the dance floor, but I could still hear the band as it eased into "Sleepy Lagoon."

It was a cluttered office, with a desk piled with papers and walls filled with photographs of men and women in uniform. They had all been smiling when their pictures were taken. I wondered how many of them were still smiling.

Bette Davis didn't offer me a seat and she didn't take one. She lit a cigarette that magically appeared from somewhere, folded her arms, and looked at me.

"I'm a private detective. Your husband . . ." I said, putting the Mah-Jongg box down on the corner of the desk.

"Farney? He . . ." Her already wide eyes opened even wider, and anger flashed. Then she pulled herself together and went on, ". . . he hired you to watch me?" There wasn't much room to pace, but she made the most of what there was.

"Watch over you," I corrected.

"Hah," she said, turning to me. "Ha and ha again. He has no reason to distrust me. I have never done anything behind my husband's back. You go back and . . . Are you smiling?"

I shrugged.

"You are smiling at me," she said.

"I said 'watch over you.' He thinks you might be in some danger."

She stopped pacing suddenly and turned to me.

"Danger?"

"Your husband is working on top-secret research," I said.

"This, as in so many scripts I have had to endure for the Brothers Warner, is redundant exposition," she said. "I am well aware that my husband is engaged in military research. He is in fact working on the modification of some kind of bombsight. And, lest you think I am giving away military secrets, Farney has frequently told people the nature of what he is working on, but not the details. Now, Mr. Peters, what has this to do with danger to me?"

She had been advancing slowly toward me as she spoke, and I had no place to go except against the wall. I stood my ground.

"I was one of the guys handling the recording the night Ham walked in on you and Howard Hughes."

The smile was gone now.

"I'm not proud of it. I didn't know what was going on. I got paid and walked away. Didn't hear anything more about it till your husband called me this morning. Your husband was contacted by someone who wanted to trade a recording for information about his work. The person who called also threatened you."

"That recording was destroyed," she said evenly.

"Not the second recording we made while your first husband was in the room with you and Hughes. The guy I was working with sold it to a small-time agent named Grover Niles, who sold it to someone else."

"Mr. Peters," she said, puffing at her cigarette. "You are quite mad. There was no second recording."

"There was," I said. "And a small-time agent named Grover Niles was murdered a few hours ago because of that record. I was with him. I'd guess he was murdered to keep me from getting to whoever has that recording."

"I appreciate your candor and confession, but what would you and Farney have me do, hide for the duration of the war?"

"Some of my friends and I will just keep an eye on you. Your husband wanted us to do it without your knowing. It won't work. We have to be close and you have to cooperate."

She looked at me for a solid thirty seconds without blinking and then crossed the room to the desk and picked up the phone. She kept looking at me when she dialed and then listened.

"For your information, Mr. Peters, I insisted on paying every penny back to Howard Hughes, every penny Ham Nelson got from him."

She hung up the phone and dialed another number.

"Hello, Farney? I'm at the Canteen. Thank you. I thought Walter Huston was wonderful too. Farney, dear, do you know a private detective named Peters?"

Most of what she did for the next ten minutes was listen.

When she finally hung up, she put out her second cigarette since entering the room and surveyed me with a new look.

"Farney is not pleased that you were unable to keep me from knowing about this," she said.

"He fire me?"

"No," she said. "He did not. He asked me to cooperate. I was not brought up to nor born to engage in blind cooperation."

"You know what I know," I said.

"I appreciate that. Well, there seems to be no help for it

other than for me to try to elude you. I haven't the energy for that. So, I will ask that you and your helpers remain as inconspicuous as possible."

I didn't bother to tell her, as I'd told her husband, that Jeremy Butler and Gunther Wherthman could not be inconspicuous.

"We'll do our best," I said.

"I appreciate your being open about this," she said, coming around the desk. "I was planning to stay here for an hour or so, but, under the circumstances, I think I'd like to go home and discuss this with my husband. He expects to be home around midnight."

"Fine with me," I said, standing away from the door so she could pass. "If it's all right with you, I'd like to make a quick stop. It's not far from here."

"Mr. Peters," she said. "I am trying to be cooperative for my husband's sake, but..."

"Brief stop. I promise."

"We live in Glendale," she said after a deep sigh.

I nodded, acknowledging the distance. She put her hand on the knob, turned to me once more, and I said, "I've got one stop to make, not far from here. All right with you if we leave your car here and pick it up later?"

"Don't forget your Mah-Jongg tiles."

Bette Davis waved, blew kisses, stroked young cheeks that had probably never been touched by a razor, and gave a variety of hugs and instructions as we moved through the crowd.

James was playing a toned-down version of "I Don't Want to Walk Without You" as we hit the door and went into the smoke-filled lobby, which suggested to Davis that she had to smoke.

When we reached it, she described my Crosley as "charming" and smiled at the old guy on the steps who was still sitting there thinking about his son and waiting for celebrities. He grinned at her and waved.

"I have never been in one of these before," she said as I pulled out of the space. "It rather reminds me of a windup toy."

I didn't answer. I turned on the radio and headed for Hoover Street and the Farraday Building while she smoked and looked out the window.

A commentator, not Keltenborn, said with glee that Major General Jimmy Doolittle had just been named president of the Massachusetts Institute of Technology Alumni Association of Japan.

"Doolittle," said the commentator with a chuckle, "was a member of the class of 1924. He replaced Takanaga Mitsui, who was in his second term. In making the announcement, the M.I.T. Alumni Association said, 'Doolittle recently dropped calling cards on Tokyo and so is well known to Japanese alumni.'"

"Please turn that off," said Davis, facing me. "Mindless ignorance offends me."

"Is there any other kind?" I asked, turning off the radio.

"Unfortunately, yes," she said. "Can you please tell me where we are going?"

"To meet my colleagues, who'll be helping to watch you and trying to find the person putting the pressure on your husband."

We didn't say much more until I was parked a few doors down from the Farraday. Even though it was a Monday night, downtown traffic was still wartime heavy.

"This is it," I said, getting out of the car and coming around to the sidewalk as she stepped out and closed the Crosley's door.

"What is it?" she asked, too sweetly.

"My office, the Farraday," I said, leading her to the big glass door and opening it for her. "Elevator's over there. We're not going to my office. I promised one of my associates I'd drop by a celebration party."

"Celebration?" she said, getting into the open elevator. "Has a dear friend been released from Folsom Prison?"

"Nope," I answered as the elevator lurched upward. "Edna St. Vincent Millay party. She got some award from the Poetry Society. Jeremy's having readings from her work, probably reading some of his own poetry."

We rattled upward into echoes and darkness.

"You are either pulling my leg, Mr. Peters, or I have underestimated you."

"Neither," I said.

The building was dark and deep. I liked the Farraday at night, the dim night lights, the creaking beams, the distant sounds of downtown, the smell of yesterdays and Lysol. It seemed haunted and sad.

The elevator lurched to a stop on the sixth floor and I opened the door to let Davis out. There were no loud noises coming from the apartment offices of Jeremy Butler and Alice Pallis Butler, but there was a hum of voices to guide us down the hall.

I didn't bother to knock. We stepped in and I closed the door behind us.

I'm not sure who was more surprised, the people celebrating who looked up and saw Bette Davis or Bette Davis who looked down and saw what must have looked to her like Saturday night at a sideshow. I'll give both sides credit. Davis simply smiled politely, and the small crowd, with one exception, tried not to gawk at her.

Jeremy stood across the room, reading aloud from a thin book.

"'While they murmured busily in the distance,'" he read, "'turning me, touching my secret body, doing what they were paid to do.'"

Jeremy closed the book. A few people applauded. Most had not heard the lines he read once Davis had entered. Jeremy stepped across the room to greet us, offering a massive hand to his guest.

"Miss Davis," he said. "I am Jeremy Butler and this is my home and that of my wife, Alice, and our baby, Natasha, who is asleep in the other room. I admire your work and am pleased to have you as a guest at our small celebration."

"I am pleased to be here," Bette Davis said. "Those lines you just read? Millay?"

"Millay," he confirmed.

"They could have been written about me after a studio fitting," she said.

"The poem is called 'The Fitting,'" Jeremy said.

Jeremy introduced the members of the group, including the three-piece-suited Gunther Wherthman, and Gwen, Alice Pallis, Sheldon Minck, and half a dozen other friends of Jeremy's—about equally divided between former wrestlers with distorted faces and massive bodies, and the poets, mostly vampire-thin and of both or unknown genders, whom Jeremy and Alice published.

"Please go on," Davis said. "I don't want to interfere."

The massive Alice had moved to Davis's side as the actress stood near the door, looking over the heads of the celebrants seated in chairs along the wall and on pillows on the floor.

"Jeremy was just about to read a poem he's written in honor of Miss Millay," Alice explained, trying not to hover over Davis.

Bette Davis smiled and glanced at me. I smiled back.

"Are you a poet, too?" asked Davis, sipping at the glass of punch Alice had handed her.

"No," said Alice, looking fondly at Jeremy. "I run the printing end. I used to print pornography, but now I'm a mother."

"On occasion I read pornography," said Davis. "And frequently I am compelled by contract to appear in celluloid obscenities."

"Would you like to read Jeremy's poem?" asked Alice shyly.

"I would love to," said Davis, stepping through the crowd

to the front of the room. Alice followed, her broad face shining.

"Toby." The voice was unmistakable, as was the odor of stale, cheap cigars.

Sheldon Minck, D.D.S., had appeared at my side. He was short, bald, with tufts of hair over his ears, thick glasses on his nose, and a cigar in his mouth. He wore a dark blazer, a white shirt with no tie, and a very happy look.

"Yeah, Shel."

"This is great, great," he said. I think he actually wrung his chubby little hands. "Mildred wouldn't come. Thought it would be dull. I gotta admit I sort of agreed with her, but I got stubborn, she got stubborn, you know how it goes."

"I know, Shel," I said, peering across the room at Bette Davis and Jeremy, deep in conversation as they looked at an open notebook Jeremy was holding.

"Wait till I tell her Bette Davis showed up," Shelly cackled with glee. "She'll have a fit. You gotta tell her. Mildred'll never believe me."

"Mildred hates me, Shel, remember."

"Hate. That's strong."

"But true, Sheldon. I don't think there's anyone in this room Mildred would believe."

Sheldon didn't look quite so happy anymore.

"I've got it," he said. "You can have Bette Davis tell Mildred. Just give her a call and . . ."

"Mildred'll think it's an imitator. She won't believe it's Bette Davis."

Imitators were a sore spot with Mildred Minck. A little over a year earlier she had run off with a Peter Lorre impersonator. He was murdered and she was a suspect. With some help from my friends, I found the killer and got Mildred off the hook. She went reluctantly back to Sheldon, for which she had never forgiven me.

"All of you gathered," Jeremy said.

"I've got it," whispered Sheldon. "A photograph. Alice has a camera. They take baby pictures. I'll get her to . . ."

"Two conditions," I whispered back.

"Miss Bette Davis has kindly agreed to read one of my poems," said Jeremy.

Enthusiastic applause as Davis smiled and nodded at me.

"What conditions?" hissed Shelly, hitching up his slipping glasses.

"I may have to call on you to help keep an eye on Miss Davis," I said. "She may be in some danger."

"Sure," he said. "Wait till Mildred hears I'll be protecting . . . wait, could I get killed?"

"Assaulting patients, getting Mildred angry, lots of ways. There's some risk."

"Okay," he said. "What other condition?"

"Mrs. Plaut has more Mah-Jongg tiles to fix. I've got them in the back seat of my car."

"How many tiles?"

"Don't know."

"Okay."

And Bette Davis began to read:

Is it not mete at this point to display
Our sincere respect for E.S.V. Millay?
While the thugs of war gnaw and flay
The light of reason burns in Millay.
In poem, or novel, essay or play,
One can count on truth from E. St. V. Millay.
There are others, false bards with meters of clay
Who pale at the prosody of Vincent Millay.
And to me thus it seems if there's more to say,
The genius to speak is Edna St. Vincent Millay.

Davis looked up and put the notebook at her side to indicate that she had finished. Jeremy, who seldom displayed emotion beyond his wife and daughter, reddened and beamed as Davis said, sincerely, "Very touching."

The room burst into applause and Shelly suddenly appeared at Davis's side, gesturing wildly to Alice Pallis, who stood near a table covered with refreshments. Alice had a camera in her hand. She took a picture of Jeremy, Bette Davis, and Sheldon Minck, who put his hand on Davis's shoulder. After a second photo, Davis talked to a few people while I made arrangements for Jeremy to relieve me on the Davis detail, and Gunther to do some digging into who might have the recording of Hughes, Davis, and Ham Nelson. I suggested he start with Andrea Pinketts and someone named Wiklund. Grover Niles had said he had sold the record to Wiklund.

A few minutes later, Davis made her way across the room to me.

"And which of these people are your colleagues who will be helping you safeguard my life and preserve what remains of my reputation?" she asked, lighting a cigarette.

I identified Jeremy, Shelly, and Gunther.

"A giant, a clown, and a dwarf," she said. "I see."

"Hold it," I said, low enough so no one could hear me. "I've worked with them for years and they know..."

"You misunderstand, Mr. Peters," she said, touching my hand. "I like them, especially the giant and his wife. I don't know if they can do their job, but they are certainly a refreshing change from the Warner dolts with whom I spend most of life. Now, I think I should like to leave."

"Three times," came a raspy voice behind me.

"I don't want to know, Juanita," I said without turning.

Bette Davis's eyes were focused over my shoulder, a decided look of amused curiosity on her face.

"Suit yourself, chum," said Juanita. "No skin off my knees."

"Please introduce us," Davis said with a smile, holding out her right hand.

There was no avoiding it. I turned and faced Juanita, a

sack of a woman in a dress that looked like a South American flag and gold earrings the size of Utah.

"Juanita," I said. "This is Bette Davis. Miss Davis, this is Juanita. She's a fortune-teller."

"A seer, honey," Juanita corrected, grabbing Bette Davis's hand and pumping it; her oversized bracelets jingled as she shook. "Parlor's on the second floor if you're ever interested. I don't make house calls, but in your case . . ."

"We've got to get going, Juanita," I said, trying to convey a strong suggestion that she let go of Davis's hand.

"That's what my second husband, Ivan, said in '26," answered Juanita. "Only he said 'I' instead of 'we.' Didn't bother me though. I knew a month before he'd wind up someplace north in jail."

"What did you mean when you told Mr. Peters 'three times'?" asked Davis, intrigued.

"No," I said.

Juanita had been right too many times in the past, and each time the information she gave me did me no good at all. Now, I don't believe in that kind of thing, but I don't disbelieve either. I just try to stay away from it.

"You'll be taken three times by a man in a mask," said Juanita. "And he'll be taken twice."

"By the man in the mask?" asked Davis.

"Yep," said Juanita. "And you know something, you've already met him. Both of you."

"Both of us have met him?" Davis asked.

"You got it, sister. Taco crumbs don't lie."

"Taco crumbs?" asked Davis, looking at me.

"Juanita can read almost anything you've touched. Tea leaves, sand, coffee grounds, taco crumbs at Manny's down at the corner."

"But I—" Davis said.

"Your hand," I said. "Let's go."

"This is fascinating," said Davis. "Can you tell me—?"

"That's it," I said.

"All I got," said Juanita with a shrug, finally dropping Bette Davis's hand and reaching over to touch her arm. "Except it's gonna start real soon. Thanks for coming, honey. And give me a call if you want to know more stuff. You're good people. I'll give you a discount."

"Thank you," said Davis as Juanita waved over her shoulder and headed for the punch bowl.

"Can we leave now?" I asked.

"Is she a little?..."

"Maybe," I said. "But you're better off not thinking too much about what she predicts."

I reached for the door but, once more, I didn't make it. Gunther had risen from the floor and, holding Gwen's hand, had advanced on us. I introduced him and Gwen to Davis. She shook their hands politely.

"Mr. Peters has told me so much about you," Davis said to Gunther. "He has great confidence in your ability."

Gwen beamed down on him proudly, and Gunther with a bow of his head said, "I am flattered."

"We've got to go now," I said.

Gwen looked as if she had something to say but couldn't quite get it out.

"It's been a pleasure," said Davis, opening the door and then, to the entire gathering, "I've enjoyed meeting you, all of you."

They indicated in return that they had enjoyed her visit, and we were about to step into the hall when Jeremy touched my shoulder and said, "Toby, you forgot something."

I didn't have to turn around. He reached over me and plunked a furry orange lump in my arms.

"Thanks," I said and stepped into the hall behind Bette Davis, who turned to look at Dash as she closed the door.

"It is important, I have discovered," she said, "to be careful not to alienate one's public. I can put in two hours of being nice, smiling, shaking hands, and making small talk, and then forget to say good-bye to someone and be labeled a snob."

"You charmed 'em," I said, ushering her down the hall.

"You really think so?"

"I'm sure," I said.

"Would you mind telling me why you are carrying a dead cat?"

"He's not dead. He's sleeping."

"Then, I take it, that is *your* cat."

"He lives with me," I conceded. "His name is Dash. He saved my life once."

"Intentionally?"

"No."

"I am reassured by his presence," said Davis as we walked in echoing Farraday darkness.

The elevator was still sitting open on the sixth-floor landing. I would have preferred to walk down and save the time, but she stepped in. I followed, closed the door, and started the ornate cell downward into the pit of shadows.

"And now, back to my car and home," she said. "I don't know how to put this, but the house is small. Our house in New Hampshire is really home. And I also maintain the houses of both Ruth, my mother, and Bobby, my sister."

"In other words, you don't have a guest room," I said.

"Not really, and I'm not sure what we would do with Nash—"

"Dash," I corrected.

"But," she went on, "we can—"

"I planned to spend the night in my car watching the house. Jeremy will relieve me in the morning so I can get some sleep and then try to find the people who have that record of you, your ex-husband, and Hughes."

The elevator bounced to a stop on the ground floor and I reached over and slid the door open.

"It has been a very long night," Davis said, stepping out.

"And it promises to be a much longer one," came a deep voice from the shadows near the exit door across the lobby.

I got in front of Davis and brushed her back, reaching for the elevator door.

"Pointless," came the voice. "You start back up and we shoot you. That elevator moves so slowly we won't even have to hurry. And believe me, folks, we have been doing a lot of hurrying tonight. Now, just step out here quietly. You give me no trouble. I give you no trouble."

We stepped out and the three men in the shadows stepped forward. The one in the middle was the shortest, about my height, and the toughest-looking.

"Name's Jeffers," he said. "My cohorts here prefer that I not give their real names. I refer to them fondly from time to time as Hans and Fritz, but I don't know if they're open to such intimacy from new acquaintances. You know what I mean?"

The cohorts were big, fugitives from Muscle Beach.

"What do you want?" Bette Davis demanded, stepping in front of me.

"What do I want?" he said with a grin. "Oh, so many things, Miss Davis. One of those big boats with guys in sailor caps who drive it around the world for you and call you captain. Or the complete attention of Ann Sheridan. Or a car like the one you are going to soon have the pleasure of taking a ride in."

"What do you want?" Davis demanded again.

"Ask Mr. Peters," said Jeffers. "I think he knows. I think he's been expecting us to call. Some business we have with your husband. And he knows I am not a man to have my wishes ignored. Do you recall our last encounter, Mr. Peters?"

Even if I hadn't remembered Jeffers, I could tell from the bruises on his face that he had recently taken a beating or a fall or a picture of Claudette Colbert in the face.

"I recall," I said.

"Then inform Miss Davis what I want."

"He wants us to go with him and give him no trouble," I said. "Remember what Juanita said? I think this is number one for both of us."

"Number... he wants us to?... He wants?" she said. "I do not care what these Three Stooges want. What *I* want is for them to go away before we are forced to call the police."

The three men advanced on us out of the shadows. No guns were showing.

"I'm armed," I tried.

"You gonna shoot us with a cat?" asked Jeffers.

Hans, the stooge on the right, held up my .38. Fritz, the stooge on the left, held up Mrs. Plaut's Mah-Jongg case.

"And what," said Bette Davis, stepping forward, hands defiantly on hips, "do you propose to do if we refuse?"

"Shoot you dead," said Jeffers.

"In that case," said Davis, "we will certainly go with you."

And we did.

Chapter Five

Comfortable?" asked Jeffers.

Davis was in the middle of the back seat. I was on one side of her with Dash sleeping in my lap. Jeffers was on the other. Hans drove while Fritz leaned over the front seat, holding a Smith & Wesson .32 automatic pointed at my chest.

"Not in the least," snapped Davis as Hans headed for the Hollywood Hills.

"Not comfortable?" said Jeffers, shaking his head. "Can you beat that, Peters? You know what you're riding in, lady?"

"A Cord convertible," snapped Davis.

"A Cord? You are sitting in the back of a Graham-Paige convertible. Only four of them ever made. Amazing vehicle. Lowest center of gravity of any American car, wider than it is high; 120 horsepower, 217.8 CID, supercharged, six-cylinder engine. No chassis. Unit body with a stub frame welded and bolted to the front end."

"I'm impressed," said Davis, with a mixture of contempt and boredom.

"You should be," said Jeffers. "But you'd rather be snotty. No offense here, but I'm not really one of your big fans."

"Nor, Mr. Jeffers, am I one of yours."

"Name's not really Jeffers," he whispered, putting a finger to his lips. "Stage name. I'm an actor. Used to be an actor. Who knows? Maybe some time . . . What's your real name?"

Davis didn't answer.

"Your name's Ruth," he said. "Ruth Elizabeth Davis. I do my research. Important in my business."

"Your business," Davis said with perfect contempt.

"He murders people," I supplied.

"If it's necessary, Tobias Leo Pevsner," said Jeffers. "But I didn't shoot Niles. Someone else had that pleasure."

We hit a pothole in the pavement as we turned off of Sunset onto one of the winding streets that lead into the hills above Los Angeles. The car bounced gently. Dash woke up and yawned.

"How do you like that?" said Jeffers. "How big was that hole, Fritz?"

"Big hole," said the driver.

"And we hardly felt it. Is this a car or is this a car?"

"It's a car," I agreed.

Dash looked around dreamily and turned his head toward Jeffers, who leaned in front of Bette Davis toward me.

"Advice, Peters," he said. "Don't be a smart ass. You cut me up and I'm not making an issue of it, but my good will can go only so far."

Dash hissed and Jeffers snapped backward.

"Keep the cat quiet or I throw him out the window," Jeffers said.

"You can try," I said. "But I don't think he likes you and he has all his teeth and claws."

Jeffers backed up further. "Just keep him quiet."

Bette Davis smiled at the rattled Jeffers and reached down in my lap to scratch Dash's head. Dash loved it.

There was no more conversation as we went up into the hills.

Below us, beyond Sunset, we could see the lights of the city. A year ago the city would have been almost dark below us, but the blackouts had been eased as the threat of Japanese invasion lessened.

Hans turned on the radio and we listened to Lanny Ross singing "Be Careful It's My Heart." Jeffers hummed along with Ross.

We were about as high up as you can get, when we pulled into the driveway of a modest one-story brick house with a great view. There were two other cars in the driveway. Fritz got out first and opened the door for me and Davis. We got out. The night had turned cool. I could feel Davis shivering at my side.

"Don't bother to look at the address, Peters," Jeffers whispered to me as he guided me toward the door. "We borrowed the place for the night. Owner's in New York on business. We didn't have time to get his permission."

I didn't say anything. On the surface, what Jeffers was saying was welcome news. He didn't care if I knew the address because it didn't matter if I led the cops back here, which might mean that he didn't plan on killing me. Why bother to advise me about not looking at the address if I was going to be dead?

On the other hand, he might just be shrewd enough to know that I'd figure this out and the information might make me less likely to give them trouble.

However, I was an eyewitness to his murdering Grover Niles and I had hit him with Claudette Colbert. But he had just told us that he hadn't shot Niles. Why bother to deny it if he was going to shoot me anyway?

I was thinking all this through when we went through the front door and were led to our right through another door and into a library where three people were sitting. Two of them I recognized. One, the woman, I didn't. The two men were seated, one in an overstuffed chair, a book in his lap, the other—Andrea Pinketts—at the end of a matching couch, a thin cigar in one hand, his legs crossed. The woman, a slightly chunky but still pretty if overly made-up blond version of Claire Trevor, stood against the bookcase looking more than a little nervous. She kept twisting the ring on her finger and looking at the man in the overstuffed chair.

"Thank you, Jeffers," the man in the overstuffed chair said. He was dressed in a dark three-piece suit with a wide, red-and-white striped tie and a matching handkerchief in his pocket. "You and your assistants may wait just outside the door."

Jeffers smiled broadly. The smile made it clear that he did not wish to stand outside any door. The smile was particularly unsettling because the light in the library was bright and the cuts on his face were red and ugly. But he and the Katzenjammer Kids left.

"You may put the cat down, Mr. Peters. Drink, Miss Davis?"

"No, thank you," she said, sitting down across from him in a straight-back chair with a padded cushion.

I put Dash on the floor. He padded off to explore the room.

"Mr. Peters?"

"Pepsi," I said, sitting a few feet from Davis in a matching straight-back chair. "Nothing for the cat."

"Inez," said the man without looking back. "A Pepsi for Mr. Peters."

"I'll have a rum collins," said Pinketts.

The man in the overstuffed chair glanced in Pinketts's direction with annoyance.

"Yes, my dear, a rum collins for our friend Mr. Pinketts."

Inez stopped playing with her ring and moved through a door next to the book-lined wall behind her. She looked relieved at the chance to escape.

"Now," said the man in the overstuffed chair, putting the

book he was holding carefully on a perfectly shined table at his side. "We can talk."

"Don't tell me," I said. "You got so tired of the noise from the Hollywood Canteen keeping you up that you decided to kidnap Bette Davis."

The last time Davis and I had seen the man in front of us was on the stoop of a house near the Hollywood Canteen. He was the older guy, the defense worker who had told me he couldn't sleep and that he had a son in the army. He was the guy who had said he spent each night waiting for a glimpse of stars so he could pass the information onto his son. He was one hell of an actor.

And then I remembered what Juanita had said, that we'd both met the man who would kidnap us. And that he had worn a mask.

"As reluctant as I am to recapitulate, Mr. Jeffers and his helpers have been following you since I contacted Mr. Farnsworth by phone yesterday. We were aware of your meeting at Levy's and we kept an eye on you while we discovered a bit more about your less-than-illustrious history. Dismissal from the Glendale Police Department. Dismissal from the Warner Brothers security staff. Divorce. Impecunious circumstances. We followed you. When you contacted Mr. Pinketts, who had initially informed us that you had knowledge of the notorious record and would make an ideal go-between, we decided to have another talk with him, and he graciously decided to cooperate with us once more."

Pinketts shrugged a *what-choice-did-I-have-amigo* shrug.

"This," the man in the overstuffed chair said, "enabled us to anticipate your visit to Grover Niles, an unsavory creature whose loss should trouble few. Though I did not in fact commit the deed, I am quite willing to take on responsibility for his demise and face judgment for it before my maker, if the ultimate irony transpires and, indeed, there is a maker."

"The Hollywood Canteen," I reminded him.

"Of course," he said. "Forgive me. I digress. We watched you searching for a parking space. I got out of the car, hurried to the front of the house in front of which you were parking, and assumed a role. My performance was, I gather, at least adequate."

"I'd rate you road company *Maid of the Ozarks*," I said.

"Underweight Sydney Greenstreet," said Davis.

"I'll accept that as praise," said the man. "My life in the theater was extensive and unrewarding. Blithering foils to Frank Fay and Skeets Gallagher. My reviews, when anyone bothered to note my performance, were patronizing. I would eventually have faded into lesser character roles until I could no longer keep the lines straight between Shakespeare and Moss Hart."

"A sad tale lacking sound and fury trying to signify something," said Davis.

"Yes, my life was a farce," said the man as Inez returned with a tray, upon which sat my Pepsi in a glassful of ice, another glass with what looked like Pinketts's rum collins, and a tumbler of beer. "I wanted tragedy and I found myself living a life of farce. I fled from comedy and turned to dealing in magic, spells, blessings, curses, and ever-filled purses."

"Gilbert and Sullivan," said Davis dryly. "I thought you were above comedy."

"Please," he said, "it is not that comedy is beneath me. It is simply not within me."

"I brought you a Schaefer," Inez said, handing the tumbler to the man. "They had Rupperts and Ballantine but I thought..."

"This will be fine, Inez."

He turned to me and Davis, held up his beer and toasted as Inez moved to the sofa to give Pinketts his drink.

"Long life and independence."

We drank.

"Wiklund," said Bette Davis.

I looked at her and she looked back at me with a triumphant smile.

"Erik Wiklund," she said.

"I am flattered," said the man, again raising his beer tumbler to her.

"Yes," she said. "I saw you in New Haven. *Underworld.* You played Bull Weed and were quite good."

Wiklund nodded his head and closed his eyes in acceptance of recognition.

"I believe you had difficulty finishing the performance," she went on, and his eyes snapped open. "Rumor had it that you were a talented man with a fondness for hard liquor."

"A fondness shared by others, including your husband, Mr. Arthur Farnsworth," he said. "I have, however, overcome my fondness, while your husband seems to have turned it into a love affair. I find I am no longer enjoying this conversation."

"There has been no conversation, Mr. Wiklund," Davis said, standing. "There has been a performance designed, I imagine, to intimidate and frighten. I find it pathetic and fourth-rate."

Pinketts looked at me and took a puff of his cigar. Inez looked frightened and twisted her ring.

"Look," I tried, seeing a look in Wiklund's eyes which held no promise of good will for me or Bette Davis.

Before I could get another word out, Wiklund picked up the book he had gently placed on the table and threw it at me. It shot past my head and hit a headless marble torso. The torso fell over but didn't break.

"The way to steal a scene is to underplay, not rant and shout," said Davis. "A lesson you obviously did not learn."

Wiklund stood up now and ran his palm across his head to smooth any gray locks which might have gone astray.

"I will call your husband now," said Wiklund. "I will tell him to get me the information I have requested. You will talk to him. I really don't care what you say. He will give me the information and I will let you go."

"With the recording," she said.

"If I am reimbursed for the money I put up to obtain it from Grover Niles, plus a modest few dollars for the investment of my time, the maintenance of my staff."

"A few dollars," Davis repeated.

"Fifty thousand," he said, pursing his lips. "I expect to get as much as two hundred thousand for the information your husband will provide. That should more than compensate for my ingenuity, the risks I have taken, and the possible charges connected to the fortunate demise of Grover Niles."

"And," said Davis, taking a step toward Wiklund. "How am I to know that there are no more copies of the record?"

"My word," said Wiklund, putting his hand to his heart.

"Arthur will not trade military secrets for my life," she said. "I would despise him if he did so and he knows it."

"Well," I said, "let's not anticipate too much here. There may be some room for negotiation, but..."

"There had best be more than some room for negotiation," said Wiklund. "Inez, tell Mr. Jeffers and his merry band to return."

Inez moved to the door and opened it. Jeffers, Hans, and Fritz stepped in.

"Now," said Wiklund, rising and moving his chair a few feet to the right. "We have a few moments of respite, a brief charade, a tribute to our captive audience."

Jeffers crossed the room to Inez, who shook her head.

"Are you familiar with *Henry the Sixth, Part Three*?" asked Wiklund.

"Can't say I am," I said.

"I was—" Wiklund said, fixing me with raised eyebrow, "—addressing Miss Davis."

"No," she said curtly.

"Pity," sighed Wiklund. "One of Shakespeare's least appreciated and seldom-done masterpieces. We are going to entertain you with a scene from this *Henry*, and when we have concluded, I would like your candid critique. Do not try to spare us."

"I assure you I will not," Bette Davis promised.

"Good," said Wiklund, pointing to where his supporting cast should stand. "Then we shall begin. Act two, scene two, Edward, Duke of York, the son of Henry, has come to take his father's throne. Backed by the Earl of Warwick and thirty thousand men, Edward confronts his father and Queen Margaret. It's a bit more complicated than that, but the drama of the moment speaks for itself. I shall play Edward, Mr. Jeffers will play Richard, and the lovely Inez will be Queen Margaret."

"Can we opt for torture instead of the performance?" asked Davis, crossing her legs.

"'She jests at scars who never felt a wound,'" Wiklund came back. And then, moving into character, "'Now, perjured Henry! wilt thou kneel for grace and set thy diadem upon my head or bide the mortal fortune of the field?'"

"'Go, rate thy minions,'" said Inez, with all the zeal of a dying trout. "'Proud insulting boy. Becomes it thee to be thus bold in terms before thy sovereign and thy lawful king?'"

"'I am his king,'" Wiklund shot back, taking a step toward Inez who looked toward Pinketts, who shrugged and puffed at his cheroot. "'And,'" Wiklund went on, "'he should bow his knee. I was adopted heir by his consent; since when, his oath is broke; for, as I hear, you that are king though he do wear the crown, to blot out me, and put his own son in.'"

"'And reason too,'" shouted Jeffers. "'Who should succeed the father but the son?'"

I had to give this to Jeffers. He was good. He sounded sincere.

"'Are you there, butcher?'" Wiklund puffed, turning to Jeffers. "'O, I cannot speak.'"

"Would that it were so," Bette Davis whispered to me.

Wiklund's eyes flicked in our direction but he went on with the show.

"'Ay, crook-back, here I stand to answer thee,'" Jeffers said angrily, teeth clenched. "'Or any he the proudest of thy sort.'"

"''Twas you that killed young Rutland, was it not?'" asked Wiklund, pointing a finger at Jeffers, who looked decidedly uncomfortable.

"'Ay,'" Jeffers shot back defensively. "'And old York, and yet not satisfied.'"

"'For God's sake, lords,'" Wiklund shouted to Hans and Fritz, who were standing at the door. "'Give signal to the fight.'"

"That will be sufficient," Bette Davis interrupted, standing. "My assessment will be painfully brief. Mr. Wiklund, with a decent director to keep your musical-hall exuberance in check, you might return to your former acceptable mediocrity. Miss Inez, your beauty is only surpassed by your ineptitude. And Mr. Jeffers, your talents are sufficient to guarantee you major character roles in the productions at Folsom Prison where you will surely reside within the month."

"Tell my agent," Jeffers said, moving to the sofa and sitting next to Pinketts.

Wiklund's eyes were fixed, unblinking with anger, at Bette Davis, who returned the gaze and went him one or two better. She looked a hell of a long way angrier than he did, but then again she was a much better actor.

Wiklund broke first.

"I suggest that Mr. Peters and Mr. Pinketts finish their drinks in the living room while Miss Davis and I call her husband. We will try to arrange, as we have planned from the beginning, an appropriate point of exchange, with Mr. Peters as go-between. If that is not possible . . . well, Miss Davis, we suggest that you be as persuasive as we know you are capable of being."

Wiklund nodded, and Hans and Fritz stepped forward to escort us, drinks in hand, out of the room.

"I'll figure something out," I whispered to Bette Davis as I moved toward the door.

"Do it quickly," she whispered back.

When Pinketts, the boys, and I were outside the door, Hans pointed with his .32 down a short corridor. We walked. Fritz was in front of us. He stopped at a door, opened it, and motioned for us to enter. Pinketts and I entered.

The windowless room was lined with shelves. The shelves were filled with thirty-five-millimeter film cans. There was a single chair and a small table in the center of the room.

Pinketts and I stepped in. Hans and Fritz stepped out and locked the door.

"I thought they were going to kill us," said Pinketts, expelling air in a rush.

"I think they plan to," I said, finishing my Pepsi and putting the empty glass on the table. "It depends on what Farnsworth tells them, and I've got the feeling he may tell them to go to hell."

"Ah," said Pinketts, "you have become an optimist."

"No," I said. "But if you don't put out that cigar, we could both become toasted hot dogs. This room is filled with film."

Pinketts reluctantly put his cigar on the floor and ground it out with his heel.

"And now," he said with a grin, sitting in the lone chair, "what is your plan?"

"I plan to stay alive," I said, moving to the nearest rack of film cans and looking at the labels.

The films, each labeled with the title and the name of the star, were in no particular order—*Hearts of Dixie, The Great K & M Train Robbery, Our Hospitality, Sunrise.*

"How?" asked Pinketts reasonably.

I began to remove the film cans from the shelves across from the door.

"Stack them in front of the door," I said. "The door opens into the room."

Pinketts shook his head.

"So you keep them out with a wall of film cans and they let us starve to death."

"Move the cans," I said, pausing to give him a grin of enormous sincerity.

"You threaten me?" he said, putting his right hand on his chest. "There are men out there planning to kill me. What have you to threaten me with?"

"No threat," I said, moving toward him and dropping the stack of full film cans in his lap. "There may be a window on the other side of the shelves. We can't move the shelves until we get the cans out."

"Then," he said, "you shall have the use of my strong back and willing arms."

Pinketts got up and stacked the cans from his lap in front of the door. It took us about ten minutes to empty the one set of shelves and stack all the cans. Then we realized that the shelves against the wall were wedged behind the two sets of shelves on the side walls. We unloaded one of those and then tried to slide the empty set out of the way. We couldn't budge it and my back started to scream.

"Keep pulling," I said.

"I do not like to sweat," said Pinketts.

"I don't like to be shot," I said.

We pulled. The shelves began to move. Not much, but they did move. It took us maybe another ten minutes to get the shelves out far enough to reach the empty shelves against the wall across from the door. That set was bigger, heavier, and there wasn't much room to move it because of the film cans covering most of the floor. When we got it far enough out, I crawled behind and found . . .

"No window."

Pinketts laughed. I came out from behind the shelves and looked at him.

"Why would anyone build a room with no window?" I asked.

"To store film or wine," said Pinketts.

"This isn't a wine room and it was built before anyone heard of movies," I said.

We both figured it out at the same time. The window was boarded over. All we had to do was tap the wall till we found it.

"We need more room," I said, stacking cans upon cans upon cans. Tom Mix on Louise Glaum on Reginald Denny.

Another ten minutes and we had enough room to inch the shelves about three feet from the wall. Finding the window was easy.

"There," I said, pointing at the place I had just tapped.

"Brilliant," said Pinketts. "Now I ask a question and you ask a question?"

"Ask."

"What do we use to make the hole?"

"I've got a better one," I said. "What do we do to cover the noise?"

"They can't get through the door," he reminded me.

"But they'll hear us breaking through the wall and be waiting for us on the other side," I said.

We moved back into what was left of the middle of the room, where I got a new idea.

"Take the tops of two cans," I said, tipping over the single chair and breaking off one thick wooden leg, which is easier to say than it was to do, especially trying not to make noise.

"When I say 'bang,'" I said, "knock them together. I'll try to go through the wall."

"Insane," said Pinketts.

I ignored him and slithered back behind the shelves with my club.

"Now," I shouted.

I hit the wall and felt the wooden chair leg go through and

hit glass, but there was no bang of cans to cover the noise I made.

"I said, 'now,'" I hissed.

"You were supposed to say 'bang,'" said Pinketts smugly on the other side of the shelves.

"What are you two doing in there?" came Jeffers's voice at the door.

"Start banging," I whispered. "And don't stop banging till I tell you."

Pinketts began to bang.

"Louder," I called as I plunged the chair leg through the wall again.

I could hear the rattle of film cans as Jeffers tried to open the door. I punched holes in the wall with a fury while Pinketts banged film-can lids and added his own touch, Italian folk songs.

It took five or six punches in the wall to get enough room to start to pull out the plaster. Jeffers had stopped trying to open the door. I knew where he was going. I worked harder.

"Bang," I shouted. "Bang for the love of Kali."

Pinketts kept banging and singing.

The good news was I made a space big enough for us to crawl through in about three wild minutes, during which I could tell that Jeffers had been joined by someone, probably Hans and Fritz, in trying to push the door open.

The bad news was that, while the window was beyond the inner wall, there was also an outer wall beyond the window.

"I'm tired," Pinketts sang out.

"I'm working," I screamed.

"They are going to move the cans," he bellowed over his own banging.

I climbed up into the space I had cleared. My back told me no, but I kept going. Then I got my back against the back of the shelving, propped the chair leg in the open space, got a grip on the top of the back of the shelves with my left hand, and kicked through the window with both feet. A sharp-toothed shock bit down my spine, but my feet went through a layer of stucco over thin plasterboard. Getting my feet back out was the trick of the night.

"Hurry," said Pinketts, banging a little more slowly.

"I'm through," I said.

"Don't give up now," cried Pinketts. "They're almost inside."

"No," I shouted, now jabbing at the stucco wall with the chair leg. "I'm through."

Andrea Pinketts renewed his din.

Sweat was stinging my eyes. I joined Pinketts in song. I was going nuts. The hole was big enough. Maybe.

"Now," I shouted.

Pinketts stopped banging, but the guys at the door pressed on. Film cans tumbled. Pinketts made his way next to me behind the bookshelf.

"You did it," he said, looking into the night through the hole.

I made a step with my hands and let him climb up and slither into the night through the hole. I wasn't sure I had enough left in my back to follow him. I clutched the club like an armed Neanderthal, leaned through the hole, and pushed my way through with my feet. I got a bonus. As I tumbled through into the night and I heard a final crash of flying film cans, the shelves behind me tipped over from my final push.

Someone inside shouted, "Shit," and I tried to roll over.

"Let's get going," I said, trying to get up.

I had a simple plan. Run to the nearest neighbor. Tell them to call the police. Do the same at two or three houses and then come back here to try to figure out a way to save Bette Davis.

I discovered several important things very quickly, things which severely changed my plans.

First, and least important, Pinketts was gone.

Second, and very important, I couldn't run. I could barely get up.

Third, and most important of all, Jeffers was standing in front of me with a gun in his hand.

"Peters, you are a dead fool," he said.

"What the hell's all the noise?" a man's voice came from the darkness behind him.

Jeffers held a finger to his lips and aimed the gun at my face.

"That you, Scott?" came another man's voice from the left. "I think it's Parrish's house."

Jeffers knelt at my side, gun to my right temple, battered face inches from mine.

"Zipper on the mouth," Jeffers whispered, making a zipper motion from left to right. "Or I shoot and run."

Someone broke through a row of bushes and I looked up at a man in his seventies wearing a blue-and-white striped bathrobe.

"Who the hell are you two?" the man asked, looking down at us.

Jeffers turned his weapon toward the man, who saw it and staggered backward.

My right hand, holding the chair leg, came up slower and not as hard as I wanted, but hard enough to catch Jeffers in the back of the head. The "klunk" was hollow. Jeffers tumbled forward and the man in the robe ran like hell.

Jeffers wasn't quite out, but he wasn't quite at home either.

He writhed around moaning as I forced myself to my knees and grabbed for his fallen gun.

That was the cue for Hans and Fritz to come running around the side of the house. They saw Jeffers on his knees, groaning, before they saw me with the gun in my hand. Hans stopped. Fritz didn't. He had a sharp-pointed white fencepost in his hands.

"Hold it," I yelled.

Fritz didn't hold it. I shot. Low. I didn't hit him but I was close enough to make Fritz stop, think, and lose his fence-post. From Hans's position, it must have been a hell of a sight. Fritz gritting his teeth by the light of the almost-full moon. Me crouched with a pistol leveled at him. Jeffers was now on his feet, dazed, looking in the wrong direction for the Melrose bus.

There were voices all around now. Neighbors. Angry voices. Frightened voices.

"I'd say you've got five minutes till the police are here," I said to Hans, who was the closest thing to leadership I could find to deal with.

On the other side of the house I could hear the gentle purr of the Graham's motor coming to life. Wiklund, Inez, and Bette Davis were going off to who-the-hell knows where, and I couldn't move.

"We'll just sit and..."

I hadn't been paying attention to Fritz, who now earned not only his Purple Heart but a gunsel's Medal of Honor. His arms were around me, squeezing, and I dropped the gun. I started to pass out from the pain but not before I heard a screeching sound.

A fuzzy orange missile flew out of the hole in the wall of the house and landed on Fritz's head.

Fritz let go of me and rolled away, but Dash tore after him, going for his face.

Another sound. A siren. Either it was an air raid or help was on the way. My last semiclear image was Hans stepping in front of me and hitting me in the face with the back of his hand. And then I was out.

I figured myself for dead. The sirens were gone. A cool breeze touched my face. The taste and smell of my own blood struck me as fascinating. I didn't want to open my eyes till I got wherever Koko the Clown, who had appeared at one side to pick me up, was taking me. He pulled some trick and had me floating in front of him. Koko pushed me as if I were a cloud, and I went sailing away like a helium-filled balloon. I liked it. It was a hell of a lot better than being beaten by killers.

Koko pointed to something in front of us. Since he was pushing my shoulders and I was lying flat, I had to look down past my shoes. I couldn't believe what I saw.

Jeremy, Gunther, Shelly, and my brother. Their hands were out to catch me. Koko pushed again and I shot forward toward them. I wanted to tell them to get out of the way, that I was going to mow them down like bowling pins. But I couldn't speak. I tried, tried to speak, tried to move as I shot ahead, feet first, the human cannonball.

I closed my eyes and waited. When there was no thud, I opened my eyes again and felt pain, in my chest, my back, my nose. I opened my eyes and saw a snarling, ancient face full of impure hate. I hoped I was wasn't looking into a mirror.

Chapter Six

This the joker?" the face in front of me said.

"Yeah," came a familiar dry voice from behind the face a few inches from my nose, breathing hellfire and garlic.

"Never saw him before," said the guy in front of me.

About this time I realized I was on my back and there was no sky beyond this guy who had never seen me before. There was only a white ceiling with a white glass fixture over a bright bulb.

"Take your time, Mr. Braddock," the voice said.

"Said I never saw him before," Braddock said, standing up.

Now I could see the guy with the dry voice. My brother Phil was sitting in a chair near the bed I was on. His head was bent forward and he was rubbing the bridge of his nose. A bad sign.

"Thank you, Mr. Braddock," Phil said.

"If I'd seen him before, I'd remember," Braddock said. "Face like that. I'd remember."

"Thank you, Mr. Braddock," Phil repeated, still rubbing his nose.

"What I want to know is why?" asked Braddock, turning to Phil, standing over him. "I want to know why and I want to know who's paying. And I goddamn sure want to know now. Sonofabitch goes loony nuts, tears holes in my house. I got a right."

"We'll get back to you, Mr. Braddock," said Phil softly.

I wanted to warn him, but decided it might be better if Phil focused his ire on Old Man Braddock rather than on me.

"Not good enough," said Braddock, leaning over Phil.

I was propped up on two pillows in the hospital bed and I could see that Braddock was big, old but big.

"Mr. Braddock," Phil said, taking his hand from his face and removing a handkerchief from his pocket to wipe his sweating palm. "I have a rotten temper. I also have a headache. I think you should get the hell out of here before my temper and headache get together. We'll get back to you."

"Braddock," I said. It came out as a sandy croak. "Run for the door. Save your life."

"What the hell do you know about it?" Braddock asked, turning to me.

"He's my brother," I said.

Braddock looked back at Phil and then at me.

"That beats all," he said. "That just about beats all. Cops and robbers holding hands. I'm gonna see Al Farlant. Believe you me. Al Farlant will hear about this in the hour."

Braddock stomped out of my hospital room and slammed the door. I missed him before the room stopped rattling. There was no one between Phil and me.

"Who the hell is Al Farlant?" I asked.

"Who gives a shit?" said Phil.

"Where's Seidman?" I asked.

"It's six in the morning," said Phil, looking at me with

tired, red eyes. "We finished our shift at two. I got to bed at three and took the call about you at five. Seidman is sleeping."

Phil walked closer to the bed and looked down at me. He shook his head in disgust.

"What?" I asked.

"Bruise on the left cheek. Bruises on half your ribs. Cuts... Someone worked you hard, Toby, but nothing's broken. You'll live. Tell me your story. Make it short and make it true."

He stood over me with his arms folded. He hadn't even bothered to put on a tie, and his jacket had a brown stain just below the pocket. I decided not to tell him about the stain.

"I was kidnapped," I said.

Phil blinked and nodded for me to go on. I did.

"Bette Davis and I were kidnapped."

Phil neither blinked nor nodded.

"The guy who shot Niles," I said. "His name, maybe not his real name, is Jeffers. He works for an ex-actor named Erik Wiklund, at least that's the name he gave us."

"Us?"

"Me and Bette Davis," I explained, reaching down to feel what I was wearing and touched a short hospital gown. They took me to the house in a Graham, locked me in the film room. I got behind the case in front of the window, made a hole with a chair leg, and got outside. They..."

"Wiklund and Jeffers?"

"No, Hans and Fritz. Not the ones in the funny papers. Two big ones with no names," I said, watching Phil's eyes. He wasn't buying any of it. "They were waiting for me. Then Jeffers came and they started to beat the hell out of me. Then, I don't know, I was here. They were gone. I..."

"No one saw anyone but you, Toby," Phil said.

"But the neighbor, he saw Jeffers with the gun."

"He says you had the gun," said Phil calmly. "You were

sitting in the backyard with a chair leg in one hand and a gun in the other, talking to yourself."

"Phil, wait, there was a woman there. I mean with Wiklund. Her name was Irene. No, Inez. And, wait. How could I forget this. Pinketts. Andrea Pinketts, the private detective. He was there."

"Hell of a party," Phil said. "All you needed was the USC cheerleaders. How did you get up there, Toby? A cab? We can check the cabs. Someone drop you?"

I laid back and closed my eyes.

"They drove us in the Graham, a convertible," I explained.

I had the sudden sensation of floating off into vast space. I opened my eyes, scared as hell. Phil was gone. I looked around the room. He was back in the chair with his head in his hand.

"Phil?" I said, trying to sit up.

It wasn't as hard as I thought.

"Phil?" I repeated.

Phil held up his free hand, a signal for me to stop.

"I didn't come here to see you, Toby," Phil said. "Ruth's been here for three days. She's on the next floor. They brought her back for more surgery. They don't know if she'll make it."

"I didn't know she was back in," I said.

"You haven't called," he said, lifting his head and sighing. "I tried to reach you."

"The boys, Lucy?" I asked, moving toward Phil on bare feet and shaky legs.

"Ruth's mother."

"Phil, I'm . . ."

"You know how much she weighs? I mean best weight on a good day. Forget about being sick, the operation."

"I don't . . ."

"Ninety pounds. You should see her now. No, you shouldn't see her now," he said, taking a deep breath. "I'm taking my leave. I've got about three months saved, maybe more. If

Ruth gets out of here, I'm staying home with her and the kids. If she . . . then I'll stay with the kids."

"If I can do anything . . ."

"You can do a lot," said Phil, looking up at me. "You can stop acting like a goddamn kid. I got enough kids. I'm not Pa."

"What I told you about last night was true," I said.

"Toby, you're not listening. I don't care if it's true. Two days ago you're with a guy who gets killed. Last night you're making holes in people's walls. I'm telling you, Toby. I just don't have the heart or gall for your shit anymore. I don't even want to talk to your client. Get dressed. Go look for the bad guys if there are any. But don't call me to save your ass next time. I won't be there. I'm turning the Niles murder over to Cawelti."

Something kicked my stomach from the inside. John Cawelti was neither brother nor pal. We hated each other. Cawelti was a big redheaded sergeant with a bad complexion, his hair parted down the middle like a barkeep, and no sense of humor.

"I'm not filing on this," said Phil, moving to the door. "I just paid a visit to my sick brother. Cawelti can book you if you're still here when he gets the call and runs over here."

"Thanks, Phil," I said.

"It doesn't matter, Tobias," he said, opening the door. "If he doesn't get you this time, he'll get you the next. Just walk through the door and find you with your big toe up your nose."

"Phil . . ." I began, but he was out in the hall, pushing the door shut behind him. He didn't slam it. Just closed it. Then he came back in.

"The gun you picked up on Niles's stairs," he said. "The one your friend Jeffers had. It didn't kill Niles. Niles was killed with a .45."

"Thanks," I said.

Phil was gone.

I found my clothes on a hook in the bathroom and got dressed, trying not to pay too much attention to the purple and yellow patches on my chest and the pain in my ribs. What with the plaster dust, grass stains, and a few tears, my pants, shirt, and jacket looked like hell. I looked in the mirror. I looked worse than hell. My right cheek was puffy and purple. There was a cut over my right eye and I needed a shave. I brushed my hair back with my hand and tried to wash my face. The left side was fine. I couldn't touch the right side.

My wallet and keys were in the night table next to the bed.

There was no cop on the door. There wouldn't be. From the way I looked, whoever dropped me here must have been sure I wouldn't be moving. Probably went down as a drunk or nut breaking into a house in the hills and making a hole in the wall.

I hit the corridor on a shift change and decided to play the bereaved visitor who had been up all night.

"Why did it have to happen to Mike?" I said, rubbing my eyes as a pair of nurses in white walked by.

They had no answer and didn't even want to deal with the problem.

I went down to the floor below using the stairway, not wanting to run into John Cawelti in case he got the good news early and decided to run over to the hospital and pay me a visit.

There were two nurses at the desk.

"Ruth Pevsner," I said.

One of the nurses, who looked as if she had been brought out of a long retirement because of the war, squinted up at me over her glasses. I knew what I looked like.

"Relative," I said.

"Relative?"

"Brother-in-law."

"No visitors," she said. "She is not conscious."

"Is she?..."

The other nurse, also in white, but young enough to be the first nurse's granddaughter, looked at me.

"Really don't know," said the nurse. "Officially, her condition is critical. Unofficially, I think she's going to make it, but... you never know. Tell a doctor I said that and I'll call you a liar."

"I won't tell a doctor," I said. "Thanks."

"You look like you need a doctor," the young nurse, plump little girl with large teeth, said.

I did something in her direction that I hoped was taken for a smile.

"I'm fine," I said. "Fell on my face running here."

Before they could think about this I walked, hands deep in my jacket pockets, to the stairway.

There was no one in the stairwell, and when I hit the main floor I opened the door a crack and looked into the corridor.

Nothing.

I stepped out and made my way toward the hospital entrance. I was watching for Cawelti or another cop I might recognize. I wasn't watching for the man in the trim beard, spectacles, and bushy hair who bumped into me.

"Many pardons," he said with a bow and a heavy German accent.

"It's okay," I said, starting to move away.

"No," he said, taking my arm. "You are not well. You should not be leaving from the hospital. You need help."

"I'll be fine," I said. "I just fell when..."

"Feel this," he said, his accent gone.

Something was jammed into my already sore ribs. His arm was around my shoulder.

"I feel it," I said.

"Guess what it is," he said.

"A gun," I said.

"Not just any gun," said Wiklund. "Your gun. I can shoot you and be out of here before anyone notices, and even if they do, the description they would give would fit a man who does not exist."

"Well?" I asked as a flurry of white uniforms went past us.

"We go out, get into the car which is waiting, and have a talk. How does that sound to you?"

"Like a great idea," I said.

We walked to the entrance, Wiklund's arm around my shoulder.

"If chance would have me king, then chance will make me king," he said. "*Macbeth.* I was just on the way up to your room when I saw you. Another few seconds either way and . . . but then Mr. Jeffers is watching the door and he surely would have seen you coming out. So . . ."

"Is she all right?"

"You shall see," he said. "You shall soon see."

And I did. The Graham was parked, engine running, about twenty feet from the hospital entrance, just far enough away to be outside the glare of the entrance lights.

"I must tell you that Mr. Jeffers and his associates are not pleased with you," Wiklund said, urging me forward toward the car with the hand barrel of the gun under his coat. "I think they would like to have a serious discussion with you."

"What do you want with me, Wiklund?" I asked.

We were almost to the car. I couldn't see inside.

"What do I want? You know my name. You know my plan. You could do enormous damage."

Wiklund nodded as two couples in hospital whites walked past us, talking about the famine in China.

"How?" I asked reasonably.

"You could give the press or the police the recording," he explained. "You could destroy the value of one of the two things we have to trade with Arthur Farnsworth, his wife and her reputation."

"So I'd ruin my client's reputation," I said, leaning forward to get into the car.

"By taking away both of our chips," he said. "You might see it as your patriotic duty. Ruin a reputation and protect a military secret. No, I cannot risk erratic behavior on your part, Peters. Please get in. My client is already having some doubts about the professionalism of my little troupe."

I got into the back seat next to Jeffers. Wiklund slid in next to me. Bette Davis was in the front passenger seat looking back at me with concern. Inez was in the driver's seat.

"Are you all right?" asked Davis.

"Considering the situation," I answered as Wiklund began to remove his makeup.

"You look terrible," Davis said. Inez stepped on the gas and started to drive.

"Maybe a nice ride will bring the pink back to my cheeks."

"This isn't funny," Davis said, looking at Jeffers and Wiklund. "They say they'll kill you if Arthur doesn't give them what they want."

I looked at Wiklund, who shrugged.

"Well," he said softly. "We can't very well kill Bette Davis, can we? If we kill you, I doubt it will make the Blue Network news, what with the war. Did you know the Japanese have launched a new battle for the Solomons?"

"No," I said.

"My goddamn head hurts," Jeffers said, looking at me. "You hit me in the face. You almost break my head. I'm beginning to run out of restraint."

"You've not treated me with great courtesy either," I reminded him.

Wiklund laughed and put an arm around my shoulder. "Peters, you are admirable. In the face of likely death, you can't stop displaying sarcasm. You should have considered a career on the stage or in film."

"I missed my calling," I said, trying to convey confidence to Bette Davis, who was still peering over the front seat with a look of alarm.

"I do not want this man harmed," she said.

"Nor do I," said Wiklund. "I like him, and he has something which belongs to me. But, my dear lady, what choice do I have? Your husband, in spite of our reasonable threats and promises, seems recalcitrant. I am afraid that I may have underestimated his patriotism. He may, it seems, prefer to sacrifice his wife's reputation and possibly her life to safeguard his country's secrets. Now, I find that admirable, but not humane or loving, and I hope I am wrong. So...would you like to supply the scenario, Mr. Peters?"

"So," I said. "He wants you to tell Arthur to give them what they want. If you don't, they'll give the recording to..."

"When you return the recording to me, Mr. Peters, we will have many options. Who knows," said Wiklund lightly. "British newspapers, Jack Warner. It could yet yield a profit and you might pass what remains of your not-very-meaningful life in peace."

"How long do you think you can keep me a prisoner before the press finds out?" Davis tried.

"Not long," admitted Wiklund. "And we don't intend to keep you. The trick is to convince your husband that you are in danger. No, I'm sorry to say that the amusing Mr. Peters is the one in quite serious trouble."

"I'm not sorry to say it," said Jeffers.

Wiklund patted my shoulder.

"We've given Mr. Farnsworth a day for an answer," Wiklund said. "Arbitrary, perhaps, but a deadline which must be met. I'd have no reputation at all in my business if my clients thought I would not deliver on threats."

"I'll call Arthur," Bette Davis said.

"Ahh," said Wiklund, sitting back.

Inez, who had said nothing, lit a cigarette and offered one to Davis, who took it and sat facing forward.

As the car filled with smoke and Inez turned the radio on, I did some quick thinking. First, the record of Davis and Howard Hughes was no longer in Wiklund's hands. For some reason, he thought I had it. Why? Answer: It had been in the house last night. Who had taken it? Jeffers, Hans, Fritz, Inez? My money, and maybe my life, was on Andrea Pinketts, who had taken off like the wind the second we had gone through the wall.

Jeffers's face was inches from mine and he was regarding me with a very small, satisfied smile.

We were heading west on Olympic toward Santa Monica, and Frank Gallop's deep voice was coming over the car radio, telling us that this was the Mutual Network and we were about to hear the "Cresta Blanca Carnival."

"C-R-E-S-T-A B-L-A-N-C-A," Gallop chanted. "Cresta." Violins. "Blanca." More violins.

The show was fine. George S. Kaufman and Oscar Levant told some jokes about the Japanese. Stu Erwin did a comic sketch about a defense-plant worker. Eileen Farrell sang an aria from *The Barber of Seville*, and Morton Gould conducted Gershwin's *Concerto in F*. We were having a swell time till we pulled onto a dark road and started up a long driveway.

The house at the end of the driveway was big, white, wooden. It looked as if it had been transported from another time and another coast.

"Nice," I said.

"Yes," said Wiklund. "Owner travels a bit, American Export Lines. Shall we go inside and make you uncomfortable?"

He got out and closed his door. Jeffers stepped out and motioned for me to follow him. Inez stepped out too. She didn't have the keys in her hand. Wiklund had his hand on the door next to Bette Davis.

"Lock that door," I whispered to Davis as I started to slide toward Jeffers who, gun in hand, was waiting for me to get out.

I didn't get out. I reached forward, slammed the door shut, pushed down the lock button, and reached over the front seat to lock the driver's door. I thought I caught a glimpse of the key in the ignition on my right and a look of horror on Inez's face out the window on my left, but I didn't have time to think about it.

"Drive," I shouted to Davis—I twisted back and locked the rear door as Wiklund reached for it.

Wiklund's face was against the window. He was no longer amused by me.

They were screaming at each other outside the car, and Jeffers did what to me seemed reasonable. He shot a hole through the rear window of the car and almost killed me. The bullet squealed and hit metal. The car lurched forward as Bette Davis hit the gas. I went down on the floor and a second shot took out the front window.

With the windows now open, I could hear their voices as a third shot thudded through the trunk of the Graham. I sat up and looked back. Davis had put some distance between the three of them and us, but we were continuing *down* the driveway toward a garage.

Help was on the way. Not for us. For the bad guys. The front door of the house opened and Hans and Fritz, who had obviously heard the noise, stepped out, armed.

The Graham stopped.

"There's no place to go," shouted Davis.

"Then back up," I said.

She threw the car in reverse and did a pretty good job of keeping it on the driveway, if you didn't place too high a value on the flowers and bushes she crushed. Wiklund and his group jumped out of the way as Bette Davis roared the Graham back up the drive.

Jeffers got off another shot, but it didn't even hit the car. Davis stopped again.

"I think I can turn around here," she said. "But that birdbath..."

She was right. There was a stone birdbath on the grass in front of the house and right in our way. She could try backing down the long twisting driveway in the dark, but we both figured that Hans, Fritz, and Jeffers had a good chance of getting to us if we tried it. There wasn't time for discussion. She gunned the Graham in first gear, slammed by the group, hit the birdbath, and lurched over it with the right-front tire. The axle groaned as we ground forward. Hans was next to the car now, reaching in for my neck. I slid back away from him as Davis changed gears again and we shot down the driveway.

I looked back through the rear window, wondering if they had another car. Maybe the Graham had emptied the communal pocketbook. All five of them were on the driveway, glaring at us and gesticulating, getting smaller as we drove. Jeffers began running after us. He had no chance of catching up, but he was giving it his best.

We hit the street and Davis skidded to avoid an oncoming car. When we were reasonably safe a few blocks away, she pulled to the side and turned to look back at me.

"Are you all right?"

"I'm alive," I said. "You?"

"Frightened, angry, tired, perspiring. What do we do now?"

"Lot of choices," I said. "We can go to the police."

"Who won't believe us," she said.

"Wiklund gave your husband a day," I said. "If he hasn't got you to bargain with and he hasn't got the record to trade, he misses his deadline. So, we call your husband, tell him you're all right and not to worry about any threats to release that record. Then we find the record before Wiklund does and, meanwhile..."

". . . we hide," she concluded.

She put the Graham in gear. The front axle was bent and we limped along, but even limping the Graham was twice the car of anything we met heading back toward Olympic.

Juanita had said I'd be kidnapped three times, and Davis twice. By my count, we both had one to go, and I didn't think Wiklund would make any mistakes the next time.

Chapter Seven

We headed for a phone at a drugstore after parking the Graham at a closed gas station on Olympic. While Bette Davis waited outside in a doorway, I called Gunther at Mrs. Plaut's, told him to forget about finding Wiklund, and to track down Pinketts. I told him I'd get back to him in the morning.

Then I bought a cheap suitcase, a pair of pajamas, a couple of toothbrushes, a big tube of Kolynos toothpaste, two coffees, an *Atlantic Monthly*, and some stale donuts to go.

We ate the donuts, drank the coffee, and caught a cab, leaving the wounded Graham for the guy who owned the gas station.

All we had to do now was hide.

It was then that I got the less-than-brilliant idea of hiding at the Great Palms Hotel on Main Street. Back in 1938 I had hidden a grifter named Albie Buttons in the Great Palms for almost a week. It was from the hotel, with Bette Davis listening, that I had called Gunther the next day and was told that he had found Pinketts.

"Pick me up in front of the Great Palms at nine," I had told him.

That had been fine with Gunther. We hung up.

"Gunther found Pinketts," I explained to Bette Davis as I waited for the operator so I could make another call.

"Then let's go get the record," she said, reaching for her handbag.

The hotel operator came on and I placed my next call, to Jeremy Butler. When I finished, I turned to Bette Davis and said, "You can't be seen."

"I'll wear a disguise," she said with exasperation. "I'll be a plump, frightened little thing with my hair pulled back and no makeup."

"*Now, Voyager,*" I said, making yet another call. "Someone will spot you."

"But—" she began.

I held up my hand to stop her when my brother picked up the phone at his house in North Hollywood and said, "Yeah."

"How is Ruth, Phil?" I asked.

"Still alive," he said, his voice flat, the voice of a man thinking about something he may have left off a grocery list. "Still alive. She lost another half pound. You believe that? She couldn't have weighed more than ninety yesterday, day before."

"Who's taking care of the kids?"

"I told you. Ruth's mom's here again," he said. "She hardly had time to get back to Iowa before she had to turn around and come back. Next time, who knows?"

"But Ruth's alive," I repeated.

"So far. As of seven-ten tonight," he said. "They won't give me odds on tomorrow or even later tonight. I just came home to lie to Ruth's mother and the kids that Ruth is doing well."

"A nurse at the hospital said she thought Ruth would make it," I said.

"Depends on which nurse you ask."

"I'm sorry, Phil," I said. "If you want me . . ."

"John Cawelti's looking for you. He missed you at the hospital."

"Phil, if you could tell him . . ."

"Toby, I don't give a shit who killed Grover Niles or why. You know why I don't give a shit?"

"Yeah," I said, watching Bette Davis pace the floor with a fresh cigarette, never taking her eyes off of me.

"Then get off the phone so I can finish here and get back to the hospital," said Phil.

I didn't say anything. He grunted and hung up.

"I'm going," I said, putting the receiver back on the cradle. "Gunther'll be downstairs in a few minutes."

She stopped pacing, folded her arms, and looked hard at me. She was wearing the dark blouse and skirt from the night before.

"I'm calling Arthur," she said, moving to the phone. "If you can do it without being listened to by the hotel operator, I—"

"She listened," I said, heading for the door. "She just doesn't understand what it means. You get on that phone and you'll have operators, clerks, morning maids, and guys from room service up here looking for your autograph."

She picked up the receiver and gave me a look of lip-twisting contempt. Then she gave a number to the hotel operator, using a vaguely Eastern European accent. It didn't sound anything like Bette Davis.

"You may leave, Mr. Peters," she said in the same accent, turning her back to me.

I hung around without bothering to pretend I had forgotten something. I just stood and listened.

"Is this there Arthur?" she said, her accent thickening.

I don't know what he said, but her side of the conversation did not make enormous sense.

"It is me," she said gleefully, her patois intact. "Elizabeth Ruth," she said. "Your vife."

Pause.

"I am just fine. And Mr. Giddins is fine also. He expect to purchase a most valuable record."

Pause, while she listened and avoided looking at me.

"If there is more than vun copy, I am sure Mr. Giddins he vill locate it."

She was looking at me with that one. I decided to make my exit.

"Fine," she said to Farnsworth. "And if Mr. Warner's assistant calls again, tell him I had to go to hotel and think some. Yah. *Gute Nacht.*"

She hung up. I was at the door again.

"Do you approve of my performance?" she asked.

"Great," I said. "Now the hotel operator thinks you're a Nazi spy."

"I shall call room service and tell them I'm Rumanian," she said.

"And how are you going to work that into the conversation?"

"Stay and listen," she said.

"Lock the door behind me," I said, and went out to meet Gunther.

He was early. In fact, he was waiting for me when I stepped out in front of the hotel. It wasn't exactly raining. More like a Los Angeles damp-rag drizzle, the kind that oozes into your clothes and weighs them down. Just enough to keep people off the streets.

Gunther drove a big black Daimler with built-up pedals. I got in and said, "Hi."

"Your face is lacerated," he said.

"I know."

"I assumed that you knew," said Gunther. "My observation was one of concern, not information."

"I'm sorry, Gunther. Let's go. I'll tell you the whole bloody tale."

"If you wish, only the salient points," he said, driving into the downtown night.

"The good parts," I said.

"Precisely."

So I told him. The drizzle turned to rain as we headed toward and eventually reached Inglewood. Gunther made a right off of Hawthorne Boulevard onto Hardy and we were in a land I didn't know.

"How the hell did you find him here?" I asked as Gunther slowed down, looking for the right house.

"As you suggested, Pinketts is not a common name. I found two of them in all of Los Angeles County. One was a Negro gentleman, Simon Pinketts. Extraordinary individual. I wish you could hear him, Toby. His Creole was precise, clear, grammatical. Of course, I do not comprehend the nuances of Creole."

"He wasn't the right one," I said.

"I'm sorry," Gunther said soberly. "I have digressed while your story was precise."

"Let's call it even, Gunther. The second Pinketts."

". . . was a relative of Andrea Pinketts. There. There is the house."

"Keep going," I said.

Gunther understood. He kept driving while I squinted through the darkness and rain at an old two-story frame house which may have once been white. Gunther found a parking space near the next corner, though we had passed several that might have been seen from the once-white house.

"To conclude," said Gunther, adjusting his glasses, "I prevailed upon the relative, a gentleman named Paul, to probe his memory for locations at which one might reasonably locate his cousin."

"Pinketts," I said, looking through the back window at the house.

"Pinketts, Andrea."

"How much did you have to give him?" I asked.

"Forty-two dollars and thirty cents," said Gunther. "He designated a bar near where he resided in Culver City."

"Nice round figure," I said.

"The amount Andrea Pinketts, his cousin, owes him."

I reached into my back pocket for my wallet and pulled it out.

"I would prefer not to be repaid for this, Toby," he said, putting his hand on the wallet.

"Client has money, Gunther."

"Your client is Bette Davis," he said.

"In a way."

"Then," he said. "It is preferable to me to do this service. I do not wish it erased."

"I never thought of you as a romantic, Gunther."

"We all change," he said.

"Gwen."

He nodded and then said, "You do not wish to go into that house?"

"I'm considering my choices here, Gunther."

"I'll be happy to accompany you."

I opened the door. The rain that had spattered on the Daimler's roof now slapped at the sidewalk.

"Let's give it fifteen minutes, Gunther," I said. "Then use your judgment."

Gunther nodded, and I got out and ran for the white house.

I was sure of three things. First, I was going to get very wet. Second, my back and cheek hurt and I belonged in a nice white hospital bed. Third, I was being very stupid. There had to be at least eight better ways of handling this.

There was one step up to a wooden porch with a leaking roof. The boards didn't creak under my feet. They just sagged like soaked cotton.

I didn't expect the door to be open and it wasn't. I could

ring the bell and there was some chance it would work, but there might be five ways out of the place, and I was in no condition to run around back and chase Pinketts who, as I remembered from the last time he took off, was pretty damn fast.

I moved to the window to the left of the door. It had a screen and the screen had jagged holes. I played with the screen. It fell off with a plop. The window was latched, but the latch was loose. I played with the window, trying to loosen the screws in the latch. They gave a little, but the window wiggled and made noise. What the hell. I pushed up steady and hard and the latch did a double somersault inside and landed on the floor. Charlie Spivak would have given me a quieter entrance.

I listened for a few seconds. Rain on the roof. Maybe something inside, but no footsteps . . . or very, very quiet ones. I put my leg through the open window, found floor, and went in. I stood still for about ten seconds and was almost sure I heard a voice. I closed the window very slowly. When it was firmly down, I was sure.

It was Pinketts.

Either the person he was talking to was very quiet or he was on the phone. It sounded like his phone voice. Everyone has a phone voice.

I needed a flashlight. The only one I had was in the Crosley, which was, I hoped, still parked in front of the Farraday. I had no idea where my .38 was, but the Buck Rogers flashlight, shaped like a space gun, had been a present from my nephews. It had almost gotten me killed when Greta Garbo . . . Pinketts raised his voice, pleading.

There was something, a thin glow, ahead of me that might have been light coming under a door. I moved toward it and Pinketts's voice. My knee hit a table or an anvil and I pulled in a deep breath.

Pinketts kept talking me toward him and I kept coming. I was close enough now to hear his end of the conversation.

"... if you think I would sell out a partner for a few hundred dollars," he said indignantly. "Pride has depth or it has no meaning. Don't threaten. I will not be panicked by reality."

I put my hand on the door and felt my way to the doorknob. The rain was slowing down outside and Pinketts was on a righteous ramble.

"Yes, yes, die," he said as I turned the knob. "I would rather die. What meaning is there in life, my enemy, if we are unable to go beyond simple sustenance and pleasure, if we sell our virtues for a luxury?"

I pushed open the door slowly, carefully, a crack that sliced light across the dark room behind me. Pinketts's voice was loud and clear now and not far away.

"Listen, of course, I'll listen," he said with a laugh. "When have you known me not to listen? Of course I would prefer to survive."

I couldn't see him but I knew he was close. On a good day, if he wasn't carrying a mace, a blowtorch, or Gatling gun, I could probably take Pinketts, especially since he was especially fond of his straight nose. But the night and the day had been hard. If I was lucky, I'd take him from behind, turn him around, and put one low in his stomach. Then, while he considered the follies of his life, I'd politely ask him for the damned record he had almost certainly stolen.

Dim light came from a lamp across the bedroom, next to a narrow canopy bed. Where the hell was he?

"Yes," he said. "But it seems I have a visitor."

I turned. He had been standing behind the door. There was no phone in his hand, but there was a bat—a runt of a bat, but big enough for this game. He swung and the bat caught me in the chest.

I fell backward and the floor hit my tailbone.

"Don't get up, Toby," Pinketts said, taking two steps forward to stand over me. He held the bat over his head in two hands. "I warn you. You have my word as a Pinketts that

I will strike and strike with a desperate fury such as only the most passionate crusaders may have known."

I had nothing to say only because I couldn't catch my breath. I went for small gulps of air and almost had time to wonder if I had added a cracked rib or two to the night's entertainment.

The bat was about a foot over my head. I could clearly see the grain and the letters burned into it: Souvenir of Lodi.

"Can you speak?" he asked.

I looked up at him. He was wearing a brown sweater with a yellow deer woven into it. The collar of his shirt under the sweater was out on the right and in on the left. The light was bad, but I had the impression that his pants were a tad wrinkled and his socks didn't match. There was no scarf around his neck and no lean cigar in his mouth. This was not the sartorial Pinketts of memory.

"Record," I gasped.

"No," he said. "The record was set no more than two months ago when another burglar entered my mother's house. I dispatched him and sent him flying with this selfsame weapon in two minutes."

"Record you stole," I growled while I hyperventilated.

"I don't have any record," he said.

"Wiklund doesn't have it," I said slowly. "It was in that house or his car. You went running off with something in your hand. I'm betting it was the record and not a bottle of Mission Bell wine."

In fact, I hadn't seen Pinketts run away and certainly hadn't seen anything in his hands, but this was the moment of truth.

"Toby, Toby," he whined, shaking his head in disappointment that his old and trusted buddy did not believe him.

"Andrea, Andrea," I answered. "Can I get up?"

"You may," he said. "I don't know if you can."

"Thanks for the grammar lesson," I said, getting to one knee.

"When English is not one's first language, one delights in the nuances," he said.

"You were born in Santa Rosa, Andrea," I said, now leaning over, hands on knees, trying to look even worse than I felt, as I breathed deeply, clenched my teeth, and rubbed my tightly taped ribs. "Your mother's name is Dixie, ran Dixie's House of Pleasure, located just behind Dixie's Bar on Rose Avenue."

I was ready for my move. Well, not really ready, but as close to it as I probably would be for the rest of the night.

"How do you know?" he asked, stepping back.

"You told me," I said. "Five years ago in the shed behind Bette Davis's house while we were waiting for her husband, Lefty."

"My mother's sleeping in the next room," Pinketts said, pointing to the door with his bat. "Keep your voice down."

I staggered a step forward, ready to grab the bat or at least block it with some part of my body other than my head or ribs. Pinketts now had a gun in his hand. I recognized it. It was mine.

"Stop," he said. "I don't want to shoot you, Toby."

"Thanks," I said.

"It would wake up my mother," he explained. "Dixie sleeps like a redwood. But a gunshot... I would prefer a quieter solution."

We were about ten feet apart.

"Question," I said. "Why'd you shoot Niles?"

"Answer," he said. "I didn't. I pride myself on my ability to deal with problems with my manner, my eloquence. I don't shoot people."

"Then," I said, taking another step forward, "what's the gun for?"

"Every person who has shot someone for the first time could have said, just moments before the act, that he had never shot anyone. I don't think it is any consolation to be the first exception to my enviable record, do you?"

"The record," I said. "I'm cold. I'm wet. My face hurts. My back hurts. My ribs hurt and I am damned mad at you. I don't want to stand around talking."

I took two steps toward him. Pinketts leveled the gun at my face.

"No," he said with a smile. "No, no, Toby. I can't let you touch me. I'm so close, so close to having enough to get out of this house, this, this..."

"The record," I said. "I want it."

"The record, the record," he hissed. "There is plenty for both of us. Wiklund will pay to get it back. He has a client who will pay, who knows, he thought a hundred thousand, maybe two. He'll pay us half that or maybe, maybe Davis's husband or Davis will pay us more? Or... who knows? The possibilities are almost endless."

"How are you going to keep Wiklund from killing us?" I said, sliding half a foot closer to him.

"I will be in a very small town on a very large beach in Chile," he said. "And when the war ends, I go back to the village of my ancestors in Rumania, buy a villa, and live like a king."

"On twenty-five thousand bucks?" I asked.

"Fifty," he said. "And we're talking about Rumania, not Paris."

"I thought we were splitting," I said, now only half-a-dozen feet away.

"Then I'll ask for more, much more," he said, showing lots of teeth. "I am not afraid of audacity."

"Give me my gun, Pinketts," I said. "You don't want to wake Dixie."

He pulled back the hammer and said softly, "There is no Dixie. My mother is dead."

It was at that moment that a voice behind Pinketts said, "Stop."

Pinketts turned toward the warning and made two mistakes. He swung the bat somewhere in the general area of where the average man's head might be, and then he fired the pistol where even a short person's stomach might reasonably be expected. The bat missed Gunther by almost a yard. The bullet, unless I was wrong, missed his head by an inch or two.

Gunther spun and threw his elbow out with a snap into Pinketts's groin. Pinketts bent over, dropped his bat and gun, and rolled over into a dresser.

"Thanks, Gunther," I said.

"Dirty," gasped Pinketts. "Dirty fighting."

"One of the few useful things I learned in my circus days," said Gunther, reaching back to help Pinketts to his feet. Pinketts scuttled back, fearing another attack.

"The record, Andrea," I said. "Tell me where it is and I'll take your word that you didn't kill Niles."

"Why?" he asked, sitting against the wall, face red, hands protecting his agony.

"Because I believe you," I said. "You shot at Gunther. You meant to kill him which means you probably meant to kill me which means you probably told me the truth when you said you didn't kill Niles because if you had you had no reason to lie since you were going to kill us anyway. You follow that, Gunther?"

"Somewhat," said Gunther, who had picked up the weapon and was now aiming it at Pinketts.

"But," said Pinketts, "I lied about my mother."

"Whose side are you on, here, Andrea? Look, someone probably heard that shot. Somebody might just have called the cops."

"It's in the room off the kitchen," he said, pointing to a door near the bed. "Records. Albums. It's in the Risë Stevens *Carmen*."

"What did you do with the *Carmen* recording?" asked Gunther.

"I threw it away," said Pinketts.

Gunther said four words in a language that might have been German, but were certainly not meant to convey approval of Pinketts's action.

"Watch him, Gunther," I said, and slouched toward the door.

I opened it, found the light switch, and looked around the room. It was stacked to the ceiling with record albums.

"Where?" I called.

"Near the window. Third shelf up, almost at the end," Pinketts answered.

I moved to the right place, reached up, and heard a gunshot. I moved as fast as I could back to the bedroom. Gunther was alone.

"I may have shot him," said Gunther, gesturing toward the open door.

I took the gun from Gunther's hand and stepped past him in time to see Pinketts go through the front door. I didn't follow him. I was too battered to catch him, and Gunther was too small.

"Let's look for that record," I said, tucking the .38 into my belt. "I'd give us five minutes, maybe less, before the police come through that door."

We looked. He took the low shelves. I took the high ones. I found the *Carmen* album in less than forty seconds, opened it, and knew that Pinketts had lied. The record clearly and commercially was labeled *Carmen*. We strewed records around. I strewed faster. Gunther didn't want to break them.

"Pons," he said, holding up an album with Lily Pons's picture on the cover. "Here it is. Not Stevens and *Carmen*. Pons and *Carmen*."

He handed the record to me. The word "Davis" was scrawled on the otherwise blank label.

"Back in the album," I said, handing it back to him.

We went out the rear door as a car pulled up in front of

the house with a wet-street squeal. There was a fence across the soggy yard.

I sloshed to it with Gunther at my side and scrambled over. I reached back for Gunther, but he just handed me the album, vaulted up, and came down next to me.

"Circus?" I asked.

"Well, perhaps I learned *two* useful things with the Ringling Brothers," he admitted.

The next step was to make our way back to Gunther's car, which took us about five minutes. We climbed in and looked back at the police car parked in front of Pinketts's house. Then Gunther pulled away from the curb.

"Invigorating," he said. "I am sorry, however, that I allowed that man to escape."

"Doesn't matter, Gunther," I said, rubbing my ribs and clutching the album. "I didn't know what to do with him anyway."

"And so," he asked. "Where?"

"To hide a record."

Gunther dropped me off at the hotel a little after midnight. I was wet, tired, in about average pain for a nearly half-century-old body that had been beaten like a Chinese gong.

The lobby was empty and Cosacos, the desk clerk who had checked Bette Davis and me in the night before, looked up from the book he was reading and registered indifference.

"Evening," I said, moving past him toward the elevator.

"Reading an interesting new book here," he said.

"That so," said I, continuing across the lobby.

"'Bout a woman who disappears," he said, a little louder.

"Sounds interesting," I said.

I was at the elevator door now. I pushed the button and watched the arrow.

"It's called *Laura*," the clerk said. "By Vera Caspary."

The arrow moved slowly down . . . 9–8–7–6—

"Humm," I said.

"Cop named McPherson falls for her. Ever hear such a thing, Mr. . . ."

What the hell was the name I had registered under?

"Giddins," I remembered.

"Yes, right," said the clerk.

5–4–3—

"Rough out there tonight," said the clerk.

2–1.

"Rough out there every night," I said, stepping into the elevator and turning to face him.

Something in my look and the swelling of my face shut him up, but I could see he was still thinking as the elevator doors closed.

I only had to knock at the door twice before Davis asked who it was.

"Me, Peters," I said.

She opened the door. She was wearing a blue shirt with long sleeves. It was a little ragged at the cuffs and collar, but it looked good on her. I wondered why I hadn't noticed her figure before, in person or on the screen.

"What have you been doing?" she asked, stepping out of the way so I could stumble in. "You look abominable."

"That may be the nicest thing anyone's said to me tonight," I said, making for the bathroom.

"What happened?" she asked.

"Tomorrow," I answered with a wave. "The morning. Now, I need a hot bath, major surgery, and something that passes for sleep. Where'd you get the shirt?"

"Hotel lost-and-found," she said. "I gave five dollars to the maid, a young woman named Florita who speaks even less English than I speak Spanish, to bring me something to wear. The result was this and several odd items now hanging in the closet, one or two of which might fit you."

"I'll take a look," I said, looking in the mirror at the face of Lon Chaney *Pere* in one of his more grotesque disguises.

"Mr. Peters," she said.

I turned to face her. She looked a little unsteady. I wasn't sure if it was her anxiety or my face.

"Have you been drinking?" she asked.

"No," I said.

"I didn't think so. I've seen too much of it to be easily mistaken. Then I assume you have been working for me and Arthur."

"Right," I said.

"And?..."

"The union endures," I said.

"Thank you, Mr. Peters."

"Call me Tobias," I said. "Almost nobody else does, except my sister-in-law and my brother, and she may not be calling me anything in a day or two."

"Family trouble?" Davis said, fishing a cigarette from the pocket of the ragged shirt and lighting it with a Zippo.

I had one hand on the frame of the bathroom door and my mind on the promise of hot water.

"My sister-in-law's name is Ruth," I said. "She's in the hospital. Probably dying. I think Ruth's about your age."

"I'm sorry," she said, and she sounded it.

"Three kids," I said. "Oldest is twelve."

"I'd like children," she said.

I looked up at her.

"You don't believe me?" she asked, holding her head up.

"I believe you," I said. "I'm just tired."

"Please keep the tap low and make a superhuman effort not to snore," she said.

I nodded and she moved to turn off the light. When I came out of the bathroom after an hour of soaking and dozing, she was in bed and breathing loudly.

What I needed was a bowl of Wheaties with milk and a lot of sugar. What I got was a too-short sofa, some memories that wouldn't leave, and a nightmare I couldn't remember when I woke up. I vaguely remembered having a brilliant insight into who might have shot Grover Niles.

The next day was uneventful. We got on each other's nerves, played cards, and eventually found ourselves where I started this tale—in the elevator of the Great Palms Hotel surrounded by Jeffers, Hans, and Fritz.

Chapter Eight

As you may recall, Bette Davis and I went quietly. I couldn't help thinking that this was my third time in their hands and Bette Davis's second. I tried to remember if Juanita had predicted anything positive. I couldn't think of anything.

We crossed the lobby with a nod to the clerk, who waved at us with his copy of *Laura*. Nobody returned his wave, but Jeffers did whisper in my ear.

"Want to hear something disgusting?" he asked, as we neared the front door.

"It's what keeps me young," I answered.

"I think I'm going to cut your ears off and feed them to Fritz," he said gently. "I'll clean them first, of course."

"You think Fritz cares if they're clean?"

"It's for me," Jeffers explained. "I mean cleanliness. I wouldn't be able to sleep thinking of his digestion . . . I've got a delicate constitution."

"Sensitive," I said, as we stepped into the night.

"I like to identify with Hamlet. You know what I mean. Vengeance, but with good taste."

"How did you find us?" I asked.

"I'll give you one guess," said Jeffers with a grin. "For a silver dollar or a box of Snickers."

"Pinketts," I guessed.

"You're a *lemac* now," Jeffers said. "That's *camel* spelled backward."

"I know. What did Pinketts say?"

"Asked if we could all be friends. Forgive and forget, if he turned you in. He said you've got the record; came to his house, tried to get him to work with you. He turned you down and then followed you to this flea trap."

"Wiklund believe that?"

"I can say, with confidence, not for a second," said Jeffers. "But then who can argue with success?"

The Graham was at the curb. It had been through almost as much body damage as I had.

"Wiklund tracked down the car in the gas station where you left it," said Jeffers. "He's not happy about its condition."

My mind was racing about as fast as a one-legged drunk, but that was fast enough to tell me that, if I got in the car, there wasn't much chance of me coming out of it alive. I was carrying the suitcase. My gun was inside it. It would take me about five seconds to get it open, find the gun... Not a chance.

Hans was standing behind Bette Davis. Fritz held the door open, and Jeffers jammed a pistol in the space just below my left ribs.

The rain had stopped. The night was cool and I was out of ideas. I decided to take a swipe at Jeffers's arm, hope he didn't hit me with his first shot, and go for the gun. Before my arm could come down, Jeffers backed away.

"No more mistakes, Peters," he said. "I can be fooled, but I'm no fool."

I looked around the street for help. And there it was. Out

of the shadows near the hotel entrance a massive figure stepped forward and lifted Jeffers by the neck.

Jeffers made a sound like "gughhh" and tried to turn his weapon on the creature behind him, which was a little difficult with his legs dangling about three inches from the ground and his face turning red. The creature held Jeffers with one hand and chopped at the gun hand with the other. The gun clattered to the sidewalk. I dropped the suitcase and moved for the gun, but Hans or Fritz had me by the shoulder and pushed me back toward the car. I hit it hard and tumbled through the open door.

Half sitting, I could see Hans let go of Bette Davis, who moved toward me.

Jeremy shook Jeffers two or three times like a wet Labrador and threw him in the general direction of Nevada. I struggled to get out of the back seat to give Jeremy a hand with Hans and Fritz, who looked like more than an uneven tag team. Jeremy was old enough to be their father. Hell, he was probably old enough to be their grandfather. Hans and Fritz had no respect for age.

Hans circled to Jeremy's left as Fritz closed in for a punch to Jeremy's stomach. Jeremy did nothing to stop the punch. Fritz's fist bounced off, and Hans leaped behind Jeremy and threw a thick arm around his neck, grabbing his own wrist and starting to pull tightly.

Jeremy looked amazingly calm as he spun around.

"Help him, for God's sake," shouted Bette Davis, trying to pull me out of the back seat.

"He's doing fine," I said.

And he was.

Jeremy was turning quickly in a circle, and Hans was lucky he had a solid grip or he would have flown into the hotel wall or over the roof of the car. Fritz tried to close in, but Hans was parallel to the ground now, about a lethal five and a half feet off the ground as Jeremy continued to spin.

Then Jeremy reached up, pulled Hans's arm from around

his neck, and brought the back of his shaved head firmly against the face of the dizzy blond Hans, who flew back and sprawled on the steps of the hotel. Fritz leaped forward, grabbing for Jeremy's head. He managed to get his fingers and nails into Jeremy's scalp, but Jeremy caught Fritz in a bear hug. Fritz was a few inches taller than Jeremy, so Jeremy had to lean back to lift him from the ground.

"I see what you mean," said Davis, watching Fritz's face go purple. "Maybe you should appeal to him before he kills them."

"No," I said, leaning against the car. "Jeremy's a pro."

Jeremy released Fritz, who crumpled to the sidewalk with a dreamy groan.

"Mr. Butler," Davis said, moving forward. "We've got to take care of your head."

There were thin streaks of red across Jeremy's scalp where Fritz had scratched him. Two of the streaks were trickling blood.

"It is of no consequence," Jeremy said, as I looked around for the gun Jeffers had lost. I didn't see it.

Far off a police siren wailed. There was a good chance it was wailing toward us.

"I have suffered worse on many occasions," said Jeremy, brushing a trail of blood from his forehead. "April 13, 1932, Nick 'The Granite' Basilica bit me on the cheek. A well-read man but with a touch of both the poet and madness. And then there was the night of June 16, 1928, New York City. Black-tie gathering. A gangster named Sharbil climbed into the ring to challenge me and brought a bottle with him."

"I think the cops are coming," I said as the sirens grew distinctly louder. "Let's talk someplace else."

"I've got a better idea," came Jeffers's voice behind us. "You and King Kong go somewhere and discuss it while the Academy Award winner and I take a ride."

We turned toward Jeffers. His hair fell madly over his

eyes, he was bent over in pain, and he was holding the gun he had dropped. He had better eyes than I did.

"I think not," said Jeremy, taking a step toward him.

Jeffers shook his head once and fired. The bullet missed Jeremy and chipped into the stone step of the hotel no more than half a foot from the confused Hans, who jumped away from the zing and splatter with a choking sound.

"One more step and you'll be working on your elegy as you wait for Saint Pete," said Jeffers.

"Colorless prose," Jeremy said.

"I'll give you the insult," said Jeffers, "but I'll take the movie star. Miss Davis, will you kindly get in the car right now or I'll shoot both of these circus freaks. I don't know why you'd care, but I'll give them the chance."

Bette Davis looked at me and Jeremy, motioned us to stay where we were, and climbed into the passenger seat of the car. The sirens were close now, maybe a block or two away. Jeffers circled the car quickly, keeping the gun leveled at us. Then he jumped in, slammed the door, and took off.

"I'm sorry, Toby," Jeremy said.

"You did great, Jeremy. I'm glad you were on the shift out here. It could have been Shelly."

The police car pulled up in front of the hotel as Jeremy rounded up Hans and Fritz and I picked up my suitcase.

The cops came out with weapons drawn. One was overage and wore thick glasses. Were it not for the war, he would have been growing oranges in Lompoc. The other cop was just a little bit older.

"We were jumped by these two," I said, pointing at Hans and Fritz. "This gentleman happened to come by and save my wallet, my suitcase, and maybe my life."

The orange-growing cop from Lompoc stepped around the police car with his gun leveled at my chest and took a look at me and then at Jeremy.

"Looks like they worked you over," he said. "We better get both of you to the emergency room."

"Sounds right to me," I said.

Fritz looked like he wanted to shoot some holes in our story, but a look from Hans shut him up. In an exchange of accusations, the Katzenjammers stood a good chance of more than unarmed robbery. They went quietly.

The emergency-room nurse patched up Jeremy's head with iodine and strips of gauze held down by tape, and then she took care of me. She was dressed in white, smelled like rubbing alcohol, and reminded me of my ex-wife, Anne. The nurse's name was Joanne Writz. Her hair was yellow, her body thin. She didn't look the least bit like Anne, but she noticed that my wounds were not fresh and she looked at me with the disapproving eyes of someone who expected no better from men.

"I saw them enter the hotel," Jeremy explained as he watched me being cleaned and chastised. "I wasn't sure it was them or I would have come inside."

"We'll find her," I said.

"You sure you want me to hear this?" asked Joanne the nurse.

"You plan to talk to anybody about it?" I asked.

"Only if I'm asked," she said, touching a rib. "Body's not bad, if you ignore the scars."

"You like movies?" I asked her.

"Sure," she said, wrapping tape around my chest.

"Judy Garland and Gene Kelly in *For Me and My Gal?*" I tried.

She looked at Jeremy and then at me.

"Are you asking me for a date?" she said, putting her hands on her hips.

"Says 'Miss' on your name tag," I answered with a grin.

"I don't go out with suicidals and children," she said.

"I'm not suicidal."

The nurse looked at Jeremy. He looked back at her and nodded.

"I'm sorry, Toby," he said. "But she may be right."

"Anne used to say I wouldn't grow up," I said, as Joanne stepped back to survey her work.

"Hmm," she said, satisfied.

"Anne's my ex-wife," I explained.

"From what I can see, she's a wise woman," said Joanne. "You can go now. Come back when you grow up. Now, if you'll please slouch out of here, I've got a gunshot, a kid with a split head, a woman who may have taken too many pills, and I'm taking orders from an eight-year-old who thinks he's an intern."

We left. It was after one and I had the beginning of an idea about finding Bette Davis.

"Where are we going?" asked Jeremy.

"You can head home, Jeremy. I'll pick up my car and some money, get a few hours' sleep, and see if I can do something without getting a friend beaten or a client's wife kidnapped."

We walked past the bleeding boy, a woman who lay on a stretcher in the hall while a sweating nurse pushed a pipe down her throat, and assorted victims with bangs and whimpers.

"You are blaming yourself too much, Toby," Jeremy observed.

"Only because I lost her. I let her get taken three times in two days," I said as we walked into the night and out of the smell of medicine. "I've got to get her back before I set a new record for losing a client in a single week."

"I'd like to help," he said as we looked for an all-night cab in front of the hospital.

"I've got something they want, Jeremy," I said. "I think I can do some trading with them."

"If you can find them," he said.

"I think maybe they'll be trying to find me," I said. A Black and White cab pulled up. "But I'm not going to wait for them."

The cab driver took a quick look at us and kept on going.

It was a nice night for a walk.

Chapter Nine

I woke up from a few hours of guilty sleep. What woke me was Mrs. Plaut clattering into my room to announce, "Mr. Peelers, a man with his hair parted down the middle, claiming to be the police, has been looking for you, and Arthur Godfrey is on the phone."

I had slept in my dirty boxer shorts and no shirt, a fact which did not seem to interest Mrs. Plaut, who looked over the room quickly to be sure I hadn't painted nude murals on the walls during the night.

"Arthur Godfrey?" I grunted over my cracked tongue as I tried to sit up, fell backward, and almost hit my head on the edge of the small table on which sat Mrs. Plaut's manuscript.

"Mr. Peelers, you look a fright, if you do not mind my saying," she said, holding up a stick she produced from behind her back. "And you have not been sleeping in your bed for two nights. If you do not mind, I must remind you that I do not cater to transients."

"When, Mrs. P.," I answered, managing to sit up in great

agony, "have you ever been the least concerned about what I minded?"

I had been certain she would not and could not hear my question, but, as so often happened in my nearly half-century of error, I was wrong.

"I was raised to politeness," she said. "And cleanliness."

With this she pointed the stick toward the corners of the room.

"Spontaneous combustion," she said.

I pulled myself up, using the sofa arm.

"The corners are so dirty that they'll suddenly break out in flame?" I grunted.

"Dirt. Dirt breeds dirt."

"Spontaneous generation, I think that is."

"Dirt breeds dirt," she repeated with satisfaction, returning her stick to her side.

I considered my crumpled trousers, an agonizing arm's length away. "Will you tell Arthur Godfrey I'm on my way? I'll be there within a generation."

"I've seen it happen," she said, straightening her blue dress with white flowers. "Room locked tight. Even a bottle locked tight. Nothing in it, nothing alive. Just some dust. Bang."

She thumped the stick down on the wooden floor, and I had to grab for the sofa arm to keep from falling.

"Bang," I said through tight teeth, as I put on my pants and wondered how long Godfrey would wait.

"Bang," she repeated, complete with thumping stick. "These little flying living things were in the bottle or wherever."

I despaired of getting a shirt or shoes on.

"Spontaneous combustion."

"Generation," I corrected.

"Life goes on."

"It's not true, Mrs. Plaut."

"Life doesn't go on? Are you an insane madman, Mr. Peelers?"

"No," I said, taking a tentative, barefooted step toward her. "Spontaneous generation. Living things from not-living things. It can't happen."

She shook her head tolerantly.

"Have you seen *Dumbo*?"

"Yes," I said.

"I think I will have seen everything when I see an elephant fly. That was a joke. But I've been around enough to have seen everything, including spontaneous..."

"... generation," I aided.

I was at the door now, inching past her. At the end of the landing a few hundred yards away I could see the telephone receiver dangling. She held her stick up in front of my face.

"Mop handle," she said.

I inspected the stick and found it a reasonable conclusion.

"It is recalcitrant," she said. "It does not yield to my attempts to reattach it to the mop head."

From behind her back, in her other hand, there came the head of a mop. I took handle and head like a good soldier as she examined my face.

"You need a poultice," she said.

The last poultice Mrs. Plaut had prepared and given me to apply to my body had been remarkably effective. It had also smelled like dead ancient underwater things, and the smell had clung lovingly to me for weeks. Pain and I were old neighbors I could live with, but the prospect of that smell, on the other hand, was not something I wanted to wear into the semicivilized land of Angeles.

Mrs. Plaut shook her head again, turned, and hurried across the landing and down the stairs.

"Peters," I said, when I finally got to the phone.

"Where is she?"

It wasn't Arthur Godfrey. It was Arthur Farnsworth.

"I don't know," I answered, looking for something besides the wall to lean on. The only thing within reach was the railing, which I didn't trust.

"They called me," he said. "A few hours ago. Bette wasn't home. They said they would let her go if I gave them the plans to the bombsight I'm working on. Peters, they know what I'm working on. That's top secret."

"And?" I prompted when he hesitated.

"And," he went on, after a deep sigh, "they want the record. They say you've got it. I give them the plans and the record and they let Bette go. Why the hell do they want the record if I give them the bombsight plans?"

"So you won't tell anyone," I said, leaning against the wall and discovering that deep breaths were not a good idea. "Makes perfect sense. They don't want you telling your boss, the FBI, anyone, that you made the trade. The record keeps you in line. It must mean their buyer raised the price he'd pay."

"I can't give them the plans," he said.

Mrs. Plaut's bird, Dexter, went wild below. There was a rattling of cage, a fluttering of feather, the voice of Mrs. Plaut shouting, "Naughty, naughty." This was followed by the bird, a yellow canary, zipping into view over the railing with a mad flutter of wings. Mrs. Plaut shouted, "Dexter, you are imperiling yourself."

"I'll get her back," I called downstairs.

"How are they getting in touch with you and when?" I asked into the receiver, as Dexter kamikazied in my general direction and then veered off toward the bathroom. Mrs. Plaut ambled back upstairs.

"They'll call at noon. That's when they'll tell me where to bring the record and the plans."

As she passed me in pursuit of Dexter, Mrs. Plaut gave me a grim look and muttered, "He is sometimes a trial and a tribulation." Then she padded down the hall in the direction of the frantic clapping of tiny wings in the bathroom.

"Agree to anything they ask," I said. "I'll call you at twelve-thirty."

"I think it's time for the FBI," Farnsworth said. "My wife's life..."

"Fine with me," I said.

"The man on the phone told me what happened, what's been going on," Farnsworth said. "And if he's even..."

"I messed up, Arthur," I said. "I let your wife get kidnapped, not once, not twice, but three times. And it gets worse, Art. I got beaten so badly I can hardly move, and the police are looking for me."

"I'm sorry, but under the circumstances..."

"Got you," squealed Mrs. Plaut triumphantly, amidst bird screeches.

"I'm calling you at half past noon," I said. "I'll have the record. You do what you have to do."

I hung up and watched Mrs. Plaut exit the upstairs bath, beaming, clasping Dexter gently in her hands. "When I was a child," she said, moving past me and down the stairs, "we had goldfish in a bowl. Brother and father were allergic to feathers and fur."

"I'm sorry to hear that," I said.

"I'll have the poultice up to you in six minutes," she called.

"That won't be—" I started, but Mrs. Plaut kicked her door and the sentence shut.

I made two more calls and then began the long treacherous journey back to my room. Half an hour later, neatly lathered in Mrs. Plaut's pungent family poultice, I stepped into the morning sun and headed for my Crosley.

"Mind if I make an observation here?" asked the turnkey with the sagging gut and ham arms, as we walked through the windowless echo of the L.A. County lockup.

"Poultice," I said.

"Poultice," he repeated.

"The smell," I explained. "Banged-up ribs. My landlady covered me with a poultice and bandaged me up."

"How's it feel?" he asked.

"Not great," I said. "But it works."

"No offense, but I wouldn't go to the dump smelling like that."

"How could anybody be offended by that observation?" I said.

Their names were Matthew Stevens and Robert Gray. Hans was Stevens. Fritz was Gray.

I found this out when the turnkey called each of them as we stood in front of their cell. There was another guy in the cell with them, a thin guy who needed a shave and coughed every fifteen or twenty seconds. The thin guy sat on the edge of a bunk and looked out at me and the turnkey with no interest in his eyes.

Lockups and prisons have their own odors. Lockups are worse. They smell like sweet old food or leftover griddle grease. I don't know why, but they all have the one smell or the other. Even Mrs. Plaut's poultice didn't completely cover that aroma.

"Which one?" asked the turnkey.

Stevens and Gray looked at each other, reasonably puzzled.

"That one," I said. "Stevens."

It was a toss-up, but I took the blond. There was something that might have been mistaken for emotion on his face.

"Right," said the turnkey, opening the cell door.

The coughing man on the cot said something no one could understand.

"What is this?" asked Stevens.

"Pal here with the perfume put up bail," said the turnkey.

"What about me?" asked Gray.

"Answer a question," I said, "and you walk with us to the plane waiting to fly your partner to Singapore. Where did Jeffers take her?"

"Take who?" asked the turnkey.

Gray shook his head slowly. "Not worth it," he said.

Stevens watched Gray and added, "I'm staying in."

"No one's asking you, Trigger," said the turnkey. "Man here wants to pay, you walk. County's not giving out vacations. Now come on out or I call for help that's not nice like yours truly."

Stevens reluctantly stepped out and looked back at Gray.

"Why're you looking at me like that?" asked Stevens. "This isn't my damned idea."

Gray turned away.

"Hey," shouted Stevens, grabbing the bars. "I'm not asking for this."

Gray snorted, his back turned. The coughing man coughed.

The turnkey pushed the door shut and nudged Stevens down the corridor.

"You'll get nothing from me," Stevens said.

"Can't hurt to try," I said.

"Yes, it can. You're walking slow," he said. "We can make you walk a lot slower."

"No," I said. "This'll do just fine, Matt. Let's go get a cup of coffee and talk about the good old days. I've got an offer that could make you rich."

We drove to Levy's on Spring. He could have jumped out at any stop. There was no way I could catch him, no way I could hold him if I did, but the suggestion of sudden wealth kept Stevens in his seat and quiet.

"How about here?" I said, parking in front of Levy's.

Stevens said nothing.

"They've got a sixty-five-cent lunch till four in the afternoon," I said.

Stevens grunted.

We got out and went into Levy's. It was a little after nine, late for the breakfast crowd, early for the lunch trade. Carmen the cashier wouldn't be on duty for another hour and a half. I sat at a table with my back to the door, and Stevens sat across from me.

"What'll it be?" said Rusty the dyspeptic waiter, his check pad at the ready. He twitched his nose as if he smelled something disagreeable, but kept it to himself. This man was a pro.

"Coffee," I said. "You got Wheaties?"

"We got Wheaties," he said.

"Wheaties," I said. "Matt?"

"Coffee," he said.

"That all?" Rusty asked, as if Stevens owed him at least the blue-plate special.

"That's all," Stevens said.

He walked toward the kitchen and I surveyed the empty tables. Someone had left a *Times* on the table next to us. I reached for it. It hurt.

"Not hungry?" I asked, looking at the headline. The U.S. had opened two drives on the Nazis in Tunisia, and Churchill was in Turkey, and the Japanese were tasting minor victory in their drive on the Solomon Islands. It was a light news day.

"You smell like puke," Stevens said.

"Flattery won't make the offer better," I said, putting the paper down.

"What offer?"

"Tell me where Jeffers and Wiklund have Bette Davis," I said. "And you walk with two hundred bucks."

Up close across the table in morning sunlight, Stevens didn't look quite as young or as stupid as he did at night.

"Two hundred dollars," he said, rubbing his chin as if he were considering the offer.

"And you walk," I said.

"I'll take it," he said.

"Good. You talk. I pay."

"I need a toilet first," said Stevens, standing as Rusty the waiter clanked down two cups of coffee.

"By the door where you come in," said Rusty the waiter.

"I saw," said Stevens, moving behind me.

I drank my coffee. It wasn't bad. Rusty hovered over the table, waiting for my reaction.

"Good, Rusty," I said. "How's it look?"

"He's going for the door now," he said.

I drank more coffee without looking back over my shoulder. I heard the door close gently, but I didn't look up or back.

"Now?"

"Cab coming down Spring. He's waving him down."

"Driver?"

"Little fat guy, bald, thick glasses, cigar," he said. "He's gettin' in."

"Got any bananas to go with the Wheaties, Rusty?"

"We got bananas, Toby."

"They gone?"

"Cab's gone," Rusty said, moving back toward the kitchen.

I finished the *Times* slowly, ate my Wheaties, left Rusty a ten-buck tip, as we had negotiated over the phone two hours earlier, and headed for my office.

I parked in an illegal space, hanging over into the crosswalk on Hoover. I had a fifty-fifty chance of making it through an hour or two without a ticket. It was worth the risk, considering my condition.

I took the elevator and listened to the sounds of the Farraday—the wails, cries, laughs, even something that sounded like a snore. Since Shelly was out driving a hack he borrowed from one of his patients who owed him for bridgework, I had to use my key to get into the office.

Something didn't feel right. The lights were off and the sun was coming through the windows. The sink was full and old dental journals were piled on the white painted-metal dental chair in the center of the room. It should have felt normal.

My office door was open. Dash came running out and stopped in front of me to meow in complaint, which I read as either: (a) I'm hungry as hell, (b) what the hell happened to you last night? or (c) something funny's going on here and you are about to find out.

All three were right.

Sergeant John Cawelti of the Los Angeles Police Department stepped into the doorway of my office. His thin red hair was parted down the middle. His pockmarked face was beaming with approaching victory. He adjusted his blue tie and said, "I can't make up my mind if you smell worse than you look."

"Take your pick," I said, not moving.

He took a step toward me. "I go for fragrant," he said. "Come on into your office and we'll have a talk."

He backed out of the way and motioned toward the open door. Dash let out a warning meow, but it was too late. I moved past Cawelti into my office and went around the desk. Dash just made it in as Cawelti closed the door. I sat slowly, carefully.

"Nice picture," he said, nodding at the Dali on the wall.

"Me and Phil," I said.

"Nice." Cawelti sat back and folded his hands.

"You booking me, John?"

He shook his head no as Dash jumped onto the desk, sending a pile of bills floating to the floor. "County attorney's office says there's enough to pull you in on suspicion of withholding information on a murder, but not enough to hold you for the deed," he said. "Could haul you for littering, taking the name of the Lord in vain, abetting a suspect to jump bail."

I reached over to rub Dash's head. He did me a favor and

allowed me to scratch. I didn't say a word. I didn't look at the phone that was now ringing.

"Matthew Stevens," Cawelti said. "Lockup a few hours ago. You posted for him. You wanna answer that?"

I picked up the phone.

"Toby?" asked Shelly Minck.

"Yes," I said, watching Cawelti's green eyes.

"It was great," Shelly said. "He had no idea. My Brooklyn accent took him in."

"Terrific," I said, smiling.

"You know where this guy wanted to go?" asked Shelly.

"Panama," I said.

"Panama?"

"How should I know where? You were driving."

"I'm doing you a favor here, Toby," Shelly said, turning sullen.

"I'm sorry," I said.

Cawelti sat forward, eyes narrowing.

"Well..."

"Can you just give me the information?" I said. "I'm having a conversation here in my office with an old friend, John Cawelti."

"The cop who..."

"Yes," I said. "Now if you'll just..."

"Who's on the other end, Peters?" asked Cawelti, getting up out of his chair and leaning toward me.

"Nice place," said Shelly. "Coldwater Canyon. Up on a hill."

He gave me the address just before Cawelti ripped the phone from my hand.

"Who is this?" he demanded.

I don't know what Shelly answered, but it didn't please Cawelti, who slammed the receiver down and leaned toward me, both palms flat on the desk. His face was turning red but he was smiling through.

"I owe you, Peters," he said, thumping a forefinger into

my sore chest. "I owe you. You made an ass of me more times than you've got hair up your ass. Your brother kept me from ripping you before, but your brother has other things on his mind now and it's just you and me."

"John," I said, rising. "I'm really enjoying this conversation. We should take more time to get together, air our feelings, exchange recipes, but I've got places to go."

Cawelti just shook his head.

"I don't have places to go?" I asked.

"Not places you want to get to. You're hurting, Peters. You could hurt a lot more. I'm a fair man. Ask anyone on the street. Hard, maybe, but fair. You tell me what the hell is going on, who you're working for, and what you know about the Niles killing. Tell me and tell me straight, and you walk without me putting a hand on you."

Cawelti stood away from the desk and showed me his palms. "My word on it," he said.

"Bygones are bygones," I said, moving around the desk and giving Dash a final head scratch.

"Let's not go that far," he said. "I'll let you walk without more pain and I'll live and let live unless you cross me. Something big's going on. I know it. I feel it. I need it, Peters."

I was face to face with Cawelti now, and there was something Irish, wild and dancing, in his green eyes.

"I've got nothing to tell you, John," I said.

He put his hand on my shoulder and found another sore spot. It didn't take much of a search. It could have been worse but it was bad enough.

"Reconsider, Toby."

He let go of my shoulder and tapped a finger against my chest. It took him almost no time to find the broken rib. My face gave me away.

"You understand where we are here?" he asked softly.

It is not a good idea to hit a cop, even if the cop is Cawelti. It can get you some bad jail time. Worse, it can get you a beating or a bullet in the stomach, but I still gave the idea some fast, serious thought. A knee to the groin, a good right to the belly, and I had a better than even chance of getting as far as the hallway, but there was no way short of breaking his legs that I'd get out of the Farraday.

Something creaked beyond my office door. Cawelti didn't hear it, but I hoped it was the cavalry.

"John," I said, raising my voice. "Since we're alone here and I don't see how anything I could say would make it worse, let me tell you that you and I have very little chance of being buddies. I know that hurts, but all you have to do is look at your face in the mirror to figure out that you do not light up a room when you enter. Now, I'm doing my best here to kiss and make up. If I'm not getting through, just give me a few pointers."

I did not like Cawelti's smile or his hand grabbing my belt.

I did like the knock at the door.

"Come in," I said.

"Get out of here," shouted Cawelti.

The door opened and my brother's partner, Steve Seidman, stepped in. That about did it for my office. Three people were definitely a crowd.

"Get out, Seidman," said Cawelti. "This is my case."

Seidman paid no attention. "Phil wants you at the hospital, Toby," he said. "Ruth's not doing so good." Then he turned to Cawelti, who still held my belt. "That is," said Seidman, "if it's all right with you, John."

Cawelti's hand was shaking as he let go. I staggered half a step back to keep from falling. Dash purred behind me and leapt onto my desk to get a better view of the action.

"Take him," he said. "We'll talk later."

I went out in front of Seidman. "You coming, John?" I asked, not wanting to leave him alone with Dash. "I'd like to lock up the office."

"I'll be along," said Cawelti, leaning against my desk.

"Citizen wants to lock his office, Sergeant," said Seidman.

"Well, then, Lieutenant," Cawelti said, following us into Shelly's office, "I think I better come back again soon."

"You do that," I said. "We'll always have a pot brewing for you."

I went with Seidman in his car, a dark Buick with leg room.

"How bad is she?" I asked.

Seidman shrugged. "They need blood. Phil gave. Says you've got Ruth's type."

We rode the rest of the way without talking. I checked my father's watch once or twice without thinking and got no information. I kept repeating the address Shelly had given me in Coldwater Canyon and wondered if I'd have time to get there before Jeffers, Wiklund, and Stevens decided to take Bette Davis somewhere else.

When we got to the hospital, I checked the lobby clock over the visitor's desk. It was almost noon. In half an hour I was supposed to call Arthur Farnsworth.

Seidman led me into a room off the emergency entrance. A young doctor in white hurried over to us. "Blood transfusion," Seidman said, nodding at me.

The kid doctor looked at me and said, "He should be lying down. I'll have to check on the blood supply and donors. Who's your doctor?" He adjusted his glasses and tried to guide me to a wheeled hospital cart.

"He's not getting blood. He's giving it," Seidman explained.

"He doesn't look very well," said the kid.

"But he's still alive," I said. "And if you have any more questions, you can point them toward me and my blood. Ruth Pevsner in 310."

"You're the brother-in-law?" he asked.

"Right."

"We've been trying to find you. Lie down. Let's get this

moving. I'll have a nurse prep you and get you up to the room."

Seidman stood back while the kid doctor stepped back and whiffed the air.

"Me," I said.

"I know," answered the doctor, moving to the door. "Anders Poultice. Great stuff. Haven't smelled it or seen it used since I was twelve, back in South Carolina. Brings back memories of my grandmother."

"My mission in life," I said.

Chapter Ten

I sometimes feel that I spend about a third of my waking time on the phone and another third on my back, a solid part of that in hospitals.

When I finished giving blood for Ruth, I got up and wobbled to the telephone in the emergency-room waiting area. The waiting room was empty except for a skinny kid about thirteen in a baseball cap, looking at a Big Little Book in a chair right in front of the phone. It was almost a quarter to one. Seidman had gone up to the third floor to be with Phil. I had told him I'd be up in a few minutes.

"You making a call?" the kid asked. I could see that the Big Little Book was *Skeezix on His Own in the Big City*, complete with flip pages. I could also see that the kid's baseball pants were rolled up and that both legs were in casts.

"Yeah."

"My mom's calling me back on that phone to pick me up."

"I won't take long."

"Fell off the back of a pop truck," he said.

"Sorry," I said.

"Broke both legs," he went on.

"Tough break," I said. I dropped my nickel in the slot, dialed Farnsworth's number, and waited half a ring before he picked up the phone.

"Mort and Walker Cooper signed with the Cards," said the kid. "You know that? Brother battery. Ain't that somethin'?"

"Sure is," I said, and then Farnsworth's voice came over the line.

"Yes?"

"Peters."

"You're late," he said.

"I'm here now," I said. "Where and when?"

"They want me to bring the plans and the record to the Hollywood Bowl at six tonight."

"Don't go," I said.

"They said..."

"I'll be there," I said, watching the kid flip pages of his book. "Besides, I've got a lead. I may be able to get your wife back before six o'clock."

The kid looked at me and the phone.

"I've got to go," I said. "I'll get back to you when I can."

I hung up and looked at the kid, who was trying to scratch under the top of his cast with a lead pencil.

"Itches," he said. "You okay? You look..."

"I'll live," I said. "Take care of yourself."

The kid didn't answer. He flipped the corners of his *Skeezix* book and half closed his eyes.

Phil and Seidman were waiting outside Ruth's room. Phil had lost his tie or shoved it in his pocket. His jacket was buttoned one button off and he needed a shave. Seidman leaned against the wall and watched.

"How is she?" I asked.

Phil ran a thick hand through his bristly gray hair and shrugged.

"They think she'll make it," he said. "Thanks for the blood. Doctor says..."

A hefty nurse came out of Ruth's room and examined us through blue horn-rimmed glasses. "One of you named Toby?" she asked, looking at us as if she wished the answer would be no.

"Me," I said.

"She wants to see you," said the nurse.

I looked at Phil, who held his hands up in resignation, and then I moved past the nurse and reached for the door. Her hand came up to hold me back.

"You smell like rotting fruit," she said.

"Poultice," I countered.

"Let him go in," said Phil.

"That's the doctor's decision," the nurse said, turning to Phil.

"That's my wife in there and this is my brother. He's going in. If you've got a doctor who doesn't like that, have him see me."

The nurse looked at Seidman, who looked at his watch, which, in contrast to mine, probably told the time.

I walked into the room, let the door close behind me, and moved to the bed.

Ruth looked like Ruth, only more so. She wasn't just thin. She looked like a lollipop stick. Her dark-yellowish hair lay sweat-wet against the pillow and her eyes peered out of little dark caves.

"Toby?" she asked, weakly trying to focus on my face.

"Toby," I agreed.

"Thanks for the blood," she said, holding out her right hand.

I moved to her side and took it. Her hand was claw-thin, white, and cold.

"It grows back fast," I said.

"I think I'm dying this time, Toby," she said evenly.

"No," I said.

"Well," she said with a sigh, "I could be wrong."

"Let's hope so," I said.

She squeezed my hand and did something with her face that might have been a smile.

"One of the bad things about probably dying," she said, "is that it's so darned hard to think of something to say that I haven't seen in a Barbara Stanwyck or Bette Davis movie."

"I'm working for Bette Davis's husband," I said.

"Really? She's my favorite," said Ruth, looking past me at the ceiling at some half-remembered Bette Davis scene.

"I know. Carmen's too," I said.

"Carmen?"

"Cashier at Levy's."

"You should get back with Anne," she said.

"Fine with me," I said.

"Tell her it was a deathbed wish of mine," said Ruth. "I miss her."

"I'll give her a call. I'm sure she'd come to see you."

"You really think I've got a chance?" she asked, focusing on my face again.

"Well, you've got reasons . . . Phil, the kids."

"I get tired, Toby," she said, turning her head away.

"I'll let you get back to sleep." I put her hand back on the bed and stepped back. "Was there something you wanted to ask me or tell me?"

"Phil doesn't take care of himself," she said.

"I know."

"He has to, now," she said, licking her cracked lips.

"You want some water?"

"I think I'd better sleep now," she said. "Tell Phil I'm not scared."

Her eyes closed and I went back into the corridor where Phil stood waiting.

"She said she's not afraid, Phil," I told him. "She's sleeping now."

"She's afraid," he said.

"I know. She doesn't want you to know. I've got to go for a few hours. I'll be back."

"I'll drive you back to your office," said Seidman, moving away from the wall.

Phil turned his back on us and went into Ruth's room. I had nothing to say to Seidman and he had nothing to say to me. He drove me to the front of the Farraday and went on his way with a "Watch out for Cawelti."

When I got up the elevator, the door to the outer office was open and the lights were on.

Shelly was sitting in his dental chair, the cabbie's cap tilted back on his shiny head, a cigar in his mouth, and his glasses perched on the end of his nose. He was wearing his white jacket and looking pleased as he put down the pamphlet he was reading.

"Anybody here?" I asked.

"Just me," Shelly said, removing his cigar and looking around to be sure he hadn't missed somebody. "At least for the next twenty minutes. Then I've got a kid coming in for extractions."

Cawelti wasn't around, which was fine with me. I had tried to think of plans, options, ideas as I drove with Seidman, but nothing came.

"You stink, Toby," he said. "If you'll pardon my French."

"I'm getting better with each passing minute," I answered, moving to my door. "You see Dash?"

"I let him in your office," Shelly said, getting out of the chair. "I got a new idea. You wanna hear?"

I didn't want to hear, but Shelly had done me a favor and I owed him one.

"Sure," I said, stepping into my office where Dash glanced up at me. The cat had been chewing up a sheet of paper. I hoped it was a bill. I moved carefully around my desk and into my chair.

"You're making funny sounds, Toby," Shelly said, sitting down in the chair across from me and adjusting his glasses.

"I'm in agony, Shel," I explained. "People keep beating the hell out of me."

"It wouldn't happen so much if you were in the health professions," he countered, without sympathy. "You wanna hear my idea or you wanna hear my idea?"

"I wanna hear your idea," I said.

"Pet dentistry."

He sat back with a smile and watched my face for a reaction.

"Pet dentistry," I repeated, looking down at Dash, who ignored me and kept chomping bills.

"Ever look in a dog's mouth?" Shelly asked.

"Shel, if you want me to take you semiseriously, either take off the hat and pretend to be a dentist or take off the smock and play cabbie."

Shelly wasn't offended. He took off the hat and placed it on my desk. "A dog's mouth?" he repeated.

"Not by choice," I said.

"They smell, Toby. Believe me. They smell and they have rotten teeth. What happens if I sink money into a storefront or a little office over some fancy-schmancy ladies' underwear shop in Beverly Hills over on Sunset? I fix the teeth of rich peoples' dogs. Make their breath smell good. Clean their teeth. Fix their cavities." Dash moved toward the cabbie's cap and Shelly whisked it away and put it on his lap.

"Did you ever work on an animal, Shel?"

"I've been reading," he answered, anticipating the question. "A couple of articles."

Maybe I was weak from donating blood, but it didn't sound like a bad idea to me. I wasn't sure Shelly was the guy to pull it off, but the idea made cockeyed sense in Los Angeles. "Sounds like it has possibilities," I said.

"Really? You think so?"

"Yeah."

"Maybe you could set up a meeting with some of those big-bucks clients you've had," beamed Shelly. "Maybe they'd

want to invest a little, tell their friends. You get fif. . . ten
percent of any client you bring in."

"I'll think about it," I said.

"I'll take care of Dash free," he said. "First patient."

"You touch that cat, Shel, and I throw you out the window."

Shelly rose from the chair indignantly and looked at the
Dali painting on the wall. "I know what I'm doing, Toby," he
said. "People don't beat the hell out of me."

"I'm sorry, Shel," I said, rubbing my forehead. "I've had a
bad day and you did me a good turn. I'll think about it.
Anything else you can tell me about the guy you picked up
in the cab?"

"Coldwater Canyon," Shelly said sulkily, hovering at the
door which he had opened. "I told you. Place is up on the
side of a hill. Old wooden place on stilts. No houses too near
it."

"He say anything?" I asked.

"Just gave me the address. Small talk. I had him conned.
You know Lochinvar Pulaski on the 'Maisie' radio show? I
did him and a little Chester Riley."

"I'm sure you were great, Shel," I said. "How are you
going to get their mouths open?"

"Who . . . oh, the dogs and cats. Knock the little bastards
out."

"Why stop at dogs and cats?" I suggested. "Why not
monkeys, rabbits, raccoons?"

"Why not?" he said, regaining his enthusiasm. "Thanks,
Toby. One more thing. You think you could talk to Mildred
about this? Tell her you think it's a good idea?"

"Your wife hates me, Shel," I reminded him.

"But she respects you."

"She doesn't respect me, Shel. She thinks I'm a bum and
should be evicted from this broom closet. She said so many
times."

Dash jumped off the desk and scooted past Shelly into his
office surgery.

"You're wrong about Mildred," he said.

"She walked out on you, Shel, with a Peter Lorre imitator. She kicked you out of the house. She tried to get all your money. She stopped you from hiring that blond receptionist."

"It was for my own good," Shelly said.

"Suit yourself, Shel, but I don't think I could convince Mildred that we are at war with the Japanese."

"She's well aware of that, believe me," said Shel.

Someone came into the outer office. Shelly heard it and turned his head.

"Patient," he said and stepped out, closing the door.

I called Jeremy's apartment one floor above, and Alice answered.

"Hi, Alice, is Jeremy in?"

"He's in the lobby, cleaning," she said. "You want to talk to Natasha?"

"Sure."

Natasha, who was a few months old, came on the phone with a crunching, slobbering sound which suggested she was chewing on the speaker. And then came, "Ahye cahbabee bee."

"You hear that?" said Alice proudly, coming back on the line.

"Smart and gorgeous," I said.

"And she needs her father," Alice added.

There was a pause while I waited for Alice's next line.

"You ask Jeremy to do some dangerous things, Toby," she said. "Do you know how old he is?"

"I—"

"Sixty-four," she answered, while Natasha cooed in her arms.

"He's the strongest—"

"Anyone can die," Alice interrupted.

"Anyone can die," I agreed. "And everyone will."

"I think Jeremy should wait his turn in line," she said.

"You're asking me? . . ."

"Nothing," she said. "He can do what he wants to do. And you can ask him to do whatever you want to ask him. I just want to make it a little harder for you to ask him."

I imagined Alice at the phone, cradling the baby in one massive arm. Alice was no beauty and she easily hit two hundred and thirty pounds on the Richter scale, but she sounded beautiful now, and I felt as lousy as I must have looked.

"Point taken, Alice."

"Good," she said. "Jeremy wrote a new poem last night. I've got it here. I want you to hear it."

In the outer office beyond the door, Shelly was singing the "Indian Love Song," which confirmed that he had a victim in the chair.

Over the phone, Alice read:

> She is all round and smooth silk to the touch
> And then she makes a sound, a motion and such
> is the miracle that is life. I smell and it is fair
> with wonder. Even her wastes are rare
> and I weep within that time is fleeing
> as I rejoice alive again through her being.
> The joy of life is that it is.
> The mystery is that it is passing.

"I get it, Alice," I said.

"Thank you," she answered. "Can you come to dinner tonight?"

"I don't think so," I said. "Another time."

"Plenty of time," she said.

I hung up and tried my best not to think about what Alice had said. The way to do that was to get moving. I got up and looked at the photograph on the wall of me, my dad, Phil, and our dog, Kaiser Wilhelm. Two kids, a skinny, pale guy in a white apron with a pained, forced smile, and a forlorn German shepherd. I wondered for the first time who had taken that picture. A neighbor? A relative? My mother had died when I was born. My old man worked fourteen-hour days in his Glendale grocery store. Was the photograph taken by some salesman? A customer? I hadn't considered the question for the almost forty years I'd had the picture, and now, suddenly, it bothered me.

I got out of my office.

Shelly was working on a girl about eight years old. The girl wore a faded dress with flowers and a look of total fear. Her mouth was wide open and her eyes darted from Shelly, who was examining his sharp, not-so-shiny tools, to me as I moved across the room.

"When I'm calling you-oo-oo-oo-oo," Shelly crooned, cleaning a giant tweezer on his jacket.

"I'll call in," I said.

Shelly didn't look in my direction. He waved a hand absently to show that he was deep in aural thought. As I closed the door, I heard him say to the kid, "You have a dog or cat?"

I hit Coldwater Canyon around three. It wasn't far from the Farraday. Finding the winding road off the Canyon Drive took a little while, but Shelly's directions were better than experience taught me they should be. The house where he had taken Matt Stevens was across the road from a sheer sheet of rock with molted boulders, a few of which were pushed off to the side. I drove past the house and found a patch in the bushes just big enough for my Crosley.

There were several approaches. I pulled my .38 out of the glove compartment, checked it, and got out, deciding on direct action rather than gamesmanship.

I made my way back to the house, staying close to the bushes and light-deprived trees, my gun ready at my side. A car announced itself and I moved away from the bushes, tucked my gun in my belt, and nodded at the driver as he weaved past me, going deeper into this bypath of Coldwater.

The house was on stilts to hold it back and up off the road, into a crevice in the hill. I climbed the wooden stairs.

On the front porch I looked around, through the windows. Nothing. That didn't mean no one was inside, only that I saw nothing. Birds were chirping and something was clacking in the bushes below. It could have been a rattlesnake.

I moved to the end of the porch, carefully looking into windows and seeing nothing but an unmade bed. I tried the first window. It wasn't locked. That didn't mean it opened quietly. It squealed and I moved slowly, carefully inching it up, watching the door inside, ready to see Jeffers or Stevens rushing in with a cackling machine gun.

No one came through that door. I got the window up and considered how best to go inside. My ribs warned me against anything stupid, and the rest of my body warned me about any movement, natural or unnatural.

The hell with it. I took a deep breath and crawled over the sill, trying to ignore the noise which, since I must say it myself, wasn't too bad. I got in, looked around, and headed for the door. I listened, heard nothing, tried the handle.

"Surprise," came Jeffers's voice.

I found myself facing Pinketts, Jeffers, and Stevens, all with weapons of various power aimed in my direction. Behind them stood Inez, biting her lower lip and not appearing to be happy with the situation, which was, at best, potentially unhealthy. "You made more noise coming in than Spike Jones and the City Slickers, and we could smell you before you opened the window."

"I've been sick," I said, keeping my gun aimed at Jeffers.

"And you sign up some pretty inept help," he said. "That cabbie was as phony as Dewey's promises. Even Matt saw through him."

There was no sign of Bette Davis or Wiklund. "I'd say we have an impasse here," I said.

"That the way you see it?" said Jeffers. "The way I see it,

it's more like a trap. We have three guns to your one, and ours are much, much bigger."

"I could shoot you before..." I began, but Jeffers was shaking his head.

"Peters, you are not one of the wisest creatures put on this earth," said Jeffers. "Far as I'm concerned, you can start shooting at any time. I'm a curious man and I'd say your chances look pretty shitty."

"Compromise," I said. "I don't put mine down. You don't put yours down. Then it's up to you if the shooting starts."

"Put it down, Toby," Pinketts said wearily, with more than a trace of ersatz Latin-lover accent. "All we want is the record back."

"Andrea," I tried. "They can't be too happy with your running away with that record and letting me get my hands on it. Let's change the odds and..."

"Mr. Pinketts and Mr. Wiklund have reached an accommodation," said Jeffers. "Mr. Pinketts led us to you last night and promised to be a good character actor in our little traveling troupe. We're all arms-around-the-neck now. Comrades. Birds of a feather. We'll throw each other birthday parties and become blood brothers."

"No Davis, no record," I said.

Jeffers shook his head and looked at Pinketts and Stevens. "Devil knows I tried," he said, holding up his gun.

"Stop it," Inez screamed suddenly behind them. "I can't stand it."

She stepped between the pointed guns and looked back and forth from me to the trio of bad guys. Her eyes were a little red and wild but they were brown and deep. Her mouth was wide and she smelled of some sweet perfume that managed to make its way through the poultice. The solid red dress she was wearing was veed down the front, and there was enough cleavage showing to grab my attention.

"No one was supposed to die," she cried. "He promised. I would come along. We'd..."

She turned to me, almost pleading, standing in line of my .38.

"... I was singing in this club in Kansas City, making a living, or almost, when Wiklund promised me the moon, the stars, and enough money to get my own bar, maybe not much of a bar, maybe in not much of a town, but something of my own. Was that a crime? I mean, after what I've been through in my life?"

She was pointing to herself now and looking at me, since none of the three on the other side of the room seemed the least interested in her story.

"I think it was a crime, Inez," I said. "Now, if you'd just step off to the side."

"No," she said defiantly, turning to face Jeffers, Pinketts, and Stevens. "No more killing."

"Get out of the way, Inez," said Jeffers, through clenched teeth.

"No," she shouted. "Shoot me. Go ahead. Shoot me. Shoot me or get out. I've had enough. I'm going back to Kansas City. You go tell Wiklund I'm going to Kansas City. He can take his promises and... So shoot me or get out."

Jeffers shook his head.

"Nothing works out, does it Peters?" he asked.

"Not usually," I agreed.

"No percentage in shooting you, Peters," Jeffers said. "We'll let Farnsworth persuade you."

He motioned Stevens and Pinketts backward toward the door. They followed. Stevens looked disappointed. Pinketts looked relieved.

"Peters," said Pinketts. "Don't be a fool."

"Why not? It makes life interesting."

And then they were gone, through the door. Out of the house. I considered aching my way after them, but what for? They didn't have Bette Davis, and I couldn't see what there was to be gained by reenacting the gunfight at the O.K. Corral.

A car started, skidded on gravel in front of the house, screeched its tires, and headed for who-the-hell-knows-where. I looked at Inez and put my gun away.

"Thanks," I said.

She shrugged and walked out of the room through a door in the rear wall. I followed her. We were in a small bedroom. There was a suitcase, a small one, on the bed. She went to the closet, took out a few slinky things and dresses, and began to fold them into the suitcase.

"You know where they have Davis?" I asked as she packed.

"I've got nothing, nothing," she sobbed. "Look at this. How am I gonna get a job? No clothes. No... I live in a suitcase I schlep around the country. Is that a life?" She turned to me, hands on hips. "You know what he promised me?"

"Wiklund?"

"Wiklund," she confirmed. "Promised me that no one would get hurt. I've been around long enough to know that it doesn't work that way."

"Whose house is this?" I asked, as she moved to the bathroom, leaving the door open.

"Who knows? Not Wiklund's. He probably just borrowed it without the owner's permission," she said with a bitter laugh.

She came out with a toothbrush and a small cloth sack with a drawstring. She threw them all in the suitcase and locked it.

"There. See? That's it. Thirty-seven years and that's all I've got to show for my life."

"I'm almost fifty and I've got even less, except for a few hundred dollars," I said. "A hundred cash as a grubstake if you tell me where Wiklund has Bette Davis."

Inez touched her hair and turned to me. "How do I look?"

"Great," I said. "Like Gene Tierney with a little meat."

"Can you give me a ride to a bus?"

"The grubstake," I reminded her. "I'll give you a ride to Union Station."

"I could lie," she said. "God knows, I've done it before, but I don't know where they've got her. They want the record. They seem to want it as much as they want the bombsight plans. They'll let her go if they get the record. There's no other way, and I suggest you give it to Wiklund. Between you and me and whatever nuthouse he was in before I met him, he has some serious wires out of place in his head. Keep that record safe if you want Bette Davis back alive."

"It's safe," I said. "In my office."

She picked up her suitcase and started to move past me.

"I can still use that ride," she said. "If not, I better start walking."

"I'll give you the ride and twenty-five bucks," I said. "Should be enough to get you to K.C."

She stopped and looked at me. "They did a real tap dance on your face," she said sympathetically. She was no more than a foot away. "I'm sorry," she added, putting a hand on my chest.

I made a face.

"I'm sorry," she said, moving her hand to my face.

"I'll live," I said. "You want to..."

She was wearing low heels that brought her almost level with me. She leaned forward and kissed me. Her mouth was open. Mine wasn't at first.

"I could use some arms around me that don't tell lies," she said, a catch in her voice.

"I'm a little tender and I smell like..."

"Hold me," she said.

I held her and wondered how close we were coming to six o'clock and the moment Farnsworth was supposed to trade the record and plans for Bette Davis. Inez's hair smelled great and her warm breasts against my chest felt even greater.

"We'd . . ." I started.

"You in a big hurry?" she asked, looking into my eyes, her face inches from mine, her skin smooth.

"Not a big one," I said.

"I'd like to leave this city with a decent memory," she said.

She put down her suitcase and came into my arms, pressing tightly against me. I staggered back and we fell onto the unmade bed. I held back a scream of pain as I almost passed out.

She was lying on top of me and I was trying to breathe but I couldn't remember how. "I'll be gentle," she said.

"I'm counting on it," I answered, pulling her down to me.

About twenty minutes later we picked up our clothes and got dressed. I never did find one of my socks. I wondered, when it came time to bill Farnsworth, if I'd charge him for new ones.

I drove Inez to Union Station. We talked on the way, a little about Wiklund, Bette Davis, the record, a lot about what she was going back to.

"It won't be so bad," she said, fishing a cigarette from her purse and lighting it. "I've got friends, or at least people I know, and I've got a good voice, but I don't kid myself, I'd never make it on radio or the movies. Now it looks like I won't even make it in the small-town saloon business. Don't take this wrong, but I'm not interested in whatever it is Farnsworth has that Wiklund wants. What say you and me just sell the record back to Farnsworth and let him trade for his wife with Wiklund?"

"I don't go that way," I said, pulling into the parking lot in front of the station.

She took a deep drag, blew out smoke, and sighed.

"With a couple thousand dollars we could spend a fun few years in a bedroom behind a bar in Bitter Creek," she said, opening the door.

"I'm a big-city kid," I said, reaching into my pocket and pulling out my wallet.

"Mistake," she said, taking the forty I handed her. She looked at it and smiled.

"Maybe," I agreed.

She leaned over and kissed me. Deep, tempting. I had a second of . . .

"See you," she said, stepping back as someone hit his horn behind me.

I pulled away and watched her in my rearview mirror as she turned and walked slowly into the train station, one light suitcase in her hand.

Chapter Eleven

We were down to the last option. I called Farnsworth from a pay phone in a gas station on Alameda, where I used up half of my remaining gas coupons. The next step would be going to No-Neck Arnie the mechanic and buying black market. I didn't want to do it, but I knew in my heart of black hearts that I would. I'd only buy a little, enough to get me by till the next ration book was issued. I'd try to buy off my conscience with a minimum purchase and a lot of lying to myself. I could do it. I had done it before, but I sure would be happy when the damned war was over and I could tell myself lies without feeling responsible for lives.

"They called," he said. "They said you almost got Bette killed."

I didn't answer. He thought things over and went on.

"It's still on. The Hollywood Bowl, but they changed the time. Now it's ten tonight. They promised to have Bette there if..."

"I'll be there," I said.

"They said I should be there alone with the record and the plans for the bombsight," he said. "Me, not . . ."

"You want to give them the plans?" I asked gently.

"No, but I don't want them to hurt her."

"What about me giving them fake plans?"

"He said they had an expert with them, the person they were planning to sell to. That person will examine the plans before the exchange is made. They may be lying. They may not be lying."

"Probably not," I said. "Stay home. I'll bring her back."

"You sound confident."

"I am," I lied.

"It's my wife's life."

"I know," I said. "She'll be home tonight."

I hung up before he could ask more questions for which I had no answers. I checked my old-man's watch. It told me I was running out of time.

On the way back to my office to pick up the record I was going to exchange, and the fake bombsight plans I was going to draw, I thought about women: Inez with her face to the window of the *Twentieth Century Limited*, looking out on fields of fruitless cornstalks and small, slow towns; Ruth in her bed, going for tough and brave and making it to scared and determined; Carmen behind the counter, living on the surface, thinking of her little boy; Anne. I imagined Anne some time just after we were married, her mouth soft, teeth white, breasts swaying, and her laugh. And then the round painted Gypsy face of Juanita tumbled in front of me and almost whispered, "Beware the ides of February."

I almost hit an ancient man in an old Ford who stopped suddenly and woke me from yesterday.

I had the feeling that I didn't smell quite so bad and I didn't ache quite so much. There wasn't much time to kill, but there was some.

Even though it was after normal office hours when I hit Hoover, there was still traffic. The war had brought out the lost, the derelict, the walking wounded. Prostitutes, the shell-shocked, the boys and girls in uniform, searching the streets for a thrill, a memory, a story to tell that made them feel they had touched life in the big bad city before they were shipped out to search in dark, deep caves for determined and deadly Japanese soldiers.

Los Angeles during the war was a fun place.

I found a parking space not far from the corner, which was fine, because I wanted to stop at Manny's. Manny specialized in tacos, but he had a varied menu which depended on what he happened to pick up at the market that morning or had left over from the decade before.

Manny's was usually open till seven or eight at night, though his real business was breakfast and lunch. The place was small, a dozen red-vinyl-topped swivel stools at the counter, half a dozen small tables against the wall. The place was narrow, but Manny maneuvered it with ample-bellied style.

There were four customers in the place when I walked in: a couple of WACs at the back table, a lone old man in a suit reading a book and eating a salami sandwich on white at another table, and Juanita at her favorite stool.

What could I do? I sat next to Juanita, who was working on a plate of tacos and a Pepsi. Juanita wasn't as gaudily attired as she had been at Jeremy and Alice's Edna St. Vincent Millay party, but she was the next best thing to a distress signal if you happened to be lost at sea. The skirt was long and purple, the blouse baggy and red with gold and silver sequins, and the earrings about the size of *H.M.S. Pinafore*.

"How's it going, Toby?" she asked. "You look like dreck."

Manny pushed away from the wall, stowed his cigarette in an ashtray at the end of the counter, and waddled in our direction.

"Thanks, Juanita. Life is treating me like a punching bag."

"But with moments," she said, pointing a long painted fingernail at my bruised face. "Moments of animal bliss."

"Do me a favor, Juanita," I said, as Manny hovered, looking bored. "Don't tell me things about my past or my future. It doesn't help."

Juanita looked at Manny in triumph. "See," she said. "He's learning. That's the trick of it, Toby. You think knowing what's coming will make it easier to deal with, but it doesn't. It just makes you feel helpless."

"Then why tell people?" I asked, looking away from her and up at Manny's bloodhound face.

"Can't help it," she said, with a jangle of her giant bracelets as she reached for a taco. "In my blood, you know? Funny thing is people *want* to know. Was I right or was I right about the three kidnappings?"

"You was right," I said.

"Couple of tacos, a Pepsi, and a coffee?" asked Manny.

"And one to go," I said.

Manny nodded and wandered back toward the small kitchen.

"Wanna know what I see for Bette Davis?"

"No," I said, pretending to look at the list of specials over the counter where the stale desserts were kept in a chiller that didn't quite work.

"Yes, you do, chum."

I said nothing.

"She doesn't have a good track record with the men," said Juanita. "And she won't. But she'll have a long life."

"Let's hope so," I said, as Manny came back with the coffee and the Pepsi.

"No hope about it, Toby. I'm the McCoy and you know it, but she wants more she'll have to come see me or, as I told her, I'll come see her. Truth is," she whispered, "the seer business is good, has been since the war. Wasn't too bad during the Depression, either. But people, kids going overseas want to know if they're gonna make it."

"What do you tell them?" I asked, sipping my Pepsi while the coffee cooled.

"Lies," she said. "Everybody who comes to me lives and comes home in one piece, whether I see it or not. Everyone gets married and lives happily ever after. Someone in uniform comes in, like those two in the back..."

I looked over at the two WACs, who were leaning toward each other and whispering.

"...I turn off the juice and try not to see anything."

"That works?"

"Sometimes," Juanita said, with a jingling shrug. "Sometimes I see what I don't want to see. Truth is, Toby, I can't just turn it on. I don't even know what it is. It comes when it wants. Some things help, like the cards or leaves. Drink your coffee."

"Don't tell me things, Juanita."

"Just a demonstration, for God's sake," she said.

"Your lipstick is smeared."

She reached for a napkin, looked at herself in the mirror behind the counter, and took care of the problem. "Drink the coffee."

I put down the Pepsi and drank some coffee. It wasn't hot. It wasn't any good either. Manny brought the three tacos, two on the plate and one on the side, wrapped in waxed paper.

Juanita and I ate our tacos in relative silence and I thought she might have forgotten or given up on looking at my coffee grounds, but I was wrong.

"You finished?" she asked, as I put the cup down and chomped on the final crispy corner of my second taco.

I grunted and she pulled the coffee cup in front of her.

"Oh, shit," she gasped loudly, after looking into the cup.

The WACs and the well-dressed old man looked over at us. Manny waddled over.

"Whatsamatter?" he asked. "Something fall into the coffee? I'll get you another one. Hold it down. I got customers."

"Sorry," Juanita said, looking up at me. "Just something I saw in the grounds."

"I like having you around," Manny whispered. "You add a little colorful *je ne sai quai*, if you know what I mean, but please don't scare the damn customers."

"Sorry, Manny," Juanita said softly.

Manny shook his head and moved away. The old man and the WACs went back to their meals.

"Don't tell me what you saw," I said.

"I can't help it, Toby. It's a damn curse. I don't know why a Jewish kid from Jersey woke up one morning and started to see things. It just happened. I had an aunt, Bess, who my cousin said had the Evil Eye, but . . ."

"What did you see in the coffee, Juanita?"

"You know."

"How many guesses do I get?" I said, gulping down the last of my taco and pocketing the one in waxed paper as I stood up.

"Sometimes I get too colorful," she said, touching my hand. "I've got nothing to do so I show off. You know what I'm doing tonight? I'm going to see the new Tyrone Power movie and then I'm going home, maybe listen to the radio, call my sister in New Jersey, and go to bed early. It's really not . . ."

"What did you see, Juanita?"

"Death," she said.

"Whose? When?"

"The lying man. It's already happened."

"Niles," I said.

"No, his name isn't Niles. I don't know what his name is, but he's the second dead man."

"What's it got to do with me?" I asked, putting a buck on the counter and finishing the Pepsi as I stood.

"The dead man is looking at you," she said. "I'm sorry."

Juanita was pale and looking at me with wide eyes. I leaned over and kissed her forehead. She smelled of something that might have been cheap lavender.

"There's more than one more, Toby," she said.

"More than one more?"

"Dead man," she said.

"Enjoy your movie," I said, moving toward the door.

It took me about four minutes from the time I left Manny's to find out what Juanita was talking about. The office was dark. I stepped in and hit the light switch in the little waiting room. It didn't work. Nothing unusual. I knew how to avoid the two chairs and the table stacked with old magazines.

I went through the door into Shelly's office and heard Dash scurrying across the floor before I found the switch.

When I turned it on, I found myself looking into the face of Andrea Pinketts, who was seated in Shelly's dental chair. Dash was sitting on Pinketts's lap, licking one paw.

Pinketts's eyes were opened in surprise and he was looking directly at me. He had one of his thin cigars dangling from his lips, waiting for a match, but there was no point in giving him a light. He was definitely not among the living.

I took the wrapped taco out of my pocket, pulled off the waxed paper, and placed it on the floor. Dash meowed and jumped down, racing for it.

I moved to the dental chair and found that Pinketts had one of Shelly's less-than-clean surgical scalpels buried deeply and professionally in the back of his neck.

Something else was wrong with the room, besides the dead and not completely cold man in the chair. To the sounds of Dash working on the taco, I did a quick survey. The place was a mess. Shelly's office was usually a disaster, but it was even worse tonight. Someone had been through it, pulling out drawers, moving cabinets.

I went to my office. The drawers were out. The Dali

picture was down and leaning against the desk. Someone had probably looked behind it. I stepped over the papers, paper clips, and assorted souvenirs of past failures and tried to think, which was no easy trick, since I almost tripped over Fritz's body on the floor behind my desk. His demise had been less clean and surgical, though it had also been from behind. His skull was crushed and bloody and the blood was still wet.

I opened my window, took in as much night air as I could handle, and sat down on my wooden chair, which someone had pushed off to the corner to make room for Fritz. I sat looking at him and around the room. I don't know how long I sat. There were no thoughts. It felt numb and relaxing and then I looked up at my door. Maybe it was a sound or just the sense.

"Toby," said Jeremy. "Are you hurt?"

I nodded my head.

"We saw the light and . . ."

"I think I just meditated, Jeremy," I said, trying to smile as he moved toward me, leaned over the desk, and saw Fritz's body.

"What happened?" he asked calmly.

"Beats hell out of me," I said, looking at Fritz for an answer.

"This is one of the men from the street," he said, examining the corpse.

"The one you shot-putted," I said.

"The other one, in the dental chair?"

"Part of the Bette Davis case," I explained. "I suppose I should get up before the cops get here. I've got a feeling whoever did this has probably called them, and a cop named Cawelti will be here grinning very soon."

"Then," said Jeremy, lifting me from the chair, "you must return to the palpable world. I suggest, if this has been arranged to implicate you and keep you from finding Miss

Davis, that Alice and I clean the suite quickly and arrange for both of the dead to be found elsewhere."

"That can get you five years, minimum," I said, rousing myself. "You and Alice. It's my problem, Jeremy."

"Frequent mayhem and murder may increase the problems of renting office space," Jeremy said, reaching down to lift Fritz's body from the floor as Alice appeared in the doorway.

"The baby is in bed," she said, looking at me.

I looked at Alice apologetically, but she was all business.

"You take the other one," Jeremy said. "We'll put them in the alley."

Alice disappeared without a word as Jeremy slung Fritz's body over his shoulder. "Not too much blood," he said. "Do what you must do, Toby. Alice and I will clean up quickly."

I should have stopped them, but I didn't. I watched Jeremy cart the body out of my office door, waited a beat or two, and then got up and went back into Shelly's office. Pinketts's body was gone and Dash had finished his taco. He sat in the dental chair cleaning himself. I leaned over, crumpled the waxed paper, and threw it toward the overflowing garbage can near the sink. It balanced precariously and didn't fall.

I moved into the waiting room, picked up the record where I'd left it under the mess of magazines on the table, and put it carefully in an empty carbon-paper box that had recently been in my bottom desk drawer but was now leaning against the wall. Then I rummaged through Shelly's strewn debris, avoiding colorful and not-so-colorful half-filled bottles and ancient pamphlets, and found some blueprint drawings of a dental x-ray machine Shelly had considered buying a year earlier. I folded them neatly, placed them in an envelope, scooped Dash up from the dental chair, and went out into the night.

Luck of a sort was with me. I pulled onto Hoover and saw the flashing lights of a police car weaving through the traffic behind me. I drove slowly, pulled over half a block down next to a fire hydrant, and turned off my lights. The police car parked in front of the Farraday and two people got out. One was a cop in uniform and the other was Cawelti.

I wondered if Alice and Jeremy would get the place cleaned up in time. I didn't wonder long. I had a movie star to rescue.

Chapter Twelve

Back in 1916 an outdoor version of *Julius Caesar* was presented with Tyrone Power, Sr., as Brutus. Spectators sat on the side of a sloping Hollywood hill with the actors below them on a low stage. It was a natural amphitheater and, according to Mr. Hill—the mailman who also lives at Mrs. Plaut's boardinghouse and claims to have been at the event—thousands attended and heard every word clearly.

The event was such a success that two years later something called *Light of Asia*, an inspirational pageant, was staged outdoors at the foot of the hills.

A series of such outdoor triumphs led Mrs. Christine Wetherill Stevenson, a far-from-broke patroness of the arts, to convince her friends to buy a chicken ranch which included a sloping hillside.

By 1926 the chicken ranch had been turned into the Hollywood Bowl, complete with stage, seats, lights, and a continuing series of concerts, plays, and inspirational events.

Anne and I, just after we were married, went to the Hollywood Bowl to see and hear John Philip Sousa's band.

After the concert we made love behind some trees near the bandstand and then stopped on the way to our apartment for chocolate sundaes at Bert's Drive-In on Sepulveda.

Well, this was another day and decade. The parking lot was closed. No surprise. I pulled over on the side of the road, told Dash to go to sleep, and picked up the envelope with the x-ray-machine plans and the record in the carbon-paper box. I also removed my .38 from the glove compartment and placed it in my jacket pocket.

There were stars out and a decently bright if not full moon. I could see well enough to make it across the long empty parking lot. The smell of poultice seemed to have deserted me, but I wasn't sure. Maybe I had just gotten used to it. My pain wasn't so bad and my ribs were sore but not throbbing. I wished I had a plan, but the memory of two bodies had dulled the joy of the night and my confidence.

The Bowl was dark and empty. The stage was bare. I was early. Suddenly I was hit by a blast of light, and a voice rang out. Wiklund's voice.

"Plenty of good seats," he shouted. "Thousands of them. Pick one."

The light went off and I tried to blink my way back to night vision but I was blind.

"Take your time, Mr. Peters," Wiklund said from the general direction of the stage.

I stood, one hand in my pocket holding my .38, the other hand clinging to my trading package.

"You may think your coming a surprise," said Wiklund from the darkness, "but it is not. To survive is to anticipate. An actor learns this early or perishes. I would have been surprised had Mr. Farnsworth shown up in person."

I could make out vague large forms now, and even had the impression of something or someone on the stage.

"When you can see sufficiently," said Wiklund, "find a seat so we can get on with the performance."

I moved slowly, cautiously, in the general direction of where I thought the front row might be.

"God, I love the resonance of this place," said Wiklund. "I'm afraid our lights will have to be minimal for this performance. Too much illumination might attract the air-raid wardens or the police. The night watchman is, unfortunately, tied up and will not be able to attend this performance, which means that we have ample time."

Two stage lights came on, not bright, but enough for me to see figures and to make my way to a front-row seat.

Wiklund, Jeffers, and Bette Davis were on stage. Davis held a champagne glass in her hand. There was a small table in the middle of the stage with an old Victrola record player perched upon it. I figured Stevens—Hans—was somewhere working the lights.

Bette Davis, dressed in a floor-length green gown glistening with a rainbow of sequins, looked in my direction—her eyes wide, her face revealing nothing. Jeffers was dressed in a tuxedo, as was Wiklund.

"You are privileged," said Wiklund. "And Mr. Jeffers and I are honored to share the stage with Miss Davis. We've been working on our lines since last night. It's only a scene, a bit of Oscar Wilde, but . . ." He shrugged. "Cucumber sandwiches with Miss Davis, who has graciously consented to appear with us, are as good as caviar with a queen."

Bette Davis forced a small smile.

"We are, unfortunately, missing a few subsidiary performers," Wiklund said as Jeffers looked at his watch and then toward me, less than lovingly. "Mr. Pinketts, Mr. Gray, and the lovely Inez are—"

"Dead," I said.

Wiklund's confidence wavered.

"I fail . . ." he began, looking at Jeffers and then at me.

"Gray and Pinketts are dead," I said, "and Inez is on her way to Jersey," I lied.

Wiklund was decidedly pale.

"You killed them?" asked Jeffers, moving forward toward the edge of the stage.

"No," I said. "I thought you people might have some idea of who killed them. I have a thought or two. Want to hear?"

Jeffers and Wiklund looked at each other, and I could see they had a thought or two of their own.

"I think whoever hired you to get these plans and this record," I said, holding up the package from under my arm, "wanted to beat you out of your cash. I think whoever hired you has come to the same conclusion I have."

"Which is?" asked Wiklund.

"That you are," said Bette Davis, stepping forward, "a company of amateurs, both as criminals and as performers."

The scene didn't look like any play I'd ever seen. I hadn't seen many plays, but I liked the way it was going, and Bette Davis and I were getting all the good lines.

"You said..." Wiklund said.

"Many things," said Davis, moving close to Wiklund, who backed away. "Many things to convince you that I planned to cooperate. But do you want to know what I think, what I've thought since I encountered you?"

She turned dramatically on Jeffers, who had moved menacingly toward her. "And you," she said. "You are suited for nothing better than low comedy. Your timing is terrible. Your voice is weak. Vaudeville, if it still existed, would reject you, and burlesque would place you at its outer fringes."

Jeffers's hand came up, but Davis proved her point about timing by throwing her drink in his face.

I put my package down on the seat next to me and applauded.

"This is all wrong," Wiklund said as Davis and Jeffers glared at each other, and wine or water dribbled down Jeffers's face. "You're lying about Pinketts and Gray."

"You've been upstaged, Wiklund," I shouted.

Someone was moving toward me out of the darkness near the stage.

"Stop it," shouted Wiklund. "You've ruined the scene, my moment."

Bette Davis had turned her back on Jeffers and was facing Wiklund again. Her hands were on her hips and she was looking at him with amused pity, a reaction he did not want to field.

"The scene is over," said Davis.

Wiklund's face was bright red. "Mr. Stevens?" he called.

"I'm here," said Stevens, stepping in front of me.

"Take the package from Mr. Peters and dispatch him," he said.

I had my gun out and pointed at Stevens's stomach as he took a step toward me. "Let Miss Davis walk down the steps and join me," I said, "or no package."

"No," shouted Wiklund. "She stays up here till I am convinced that you have given me the genuine article."

"Impasse again," I said.

"Hell, no," said Jeffers, pulling a gun out of his tux and aiming it at Davis.

I handed the package to Stevens, who grinned, took it, turned his back on me and my weapon, and moved to the edge of the stage where Wiklund came forward to take it.

Wiklund moved to the Victrola, tore open the carbon-paper box, and placed the record on the machine. He hit a switch and stood back. The speaker crackled and the needle picked up the first scratches before the voice of Kate Smith burst out with "God Bless America."

Things moved fast now. Bette Davis kicked Jeffers between the legs. The gun in his hand went off, sending a wild bullet into the Victrola and cutting Kate Smith off in mid "land that I love." Davis took Jeffers's gun hand and bit it. The gun fell to the stage. Davis tried another kick at the bent-over Jeffers, but his arm went out and he blocked it as he went to his knees groping for his gun.

Wiklund hesitated, but Stevens turned toward me and

reached into his jacket. Before he could get it out a shot went off, echoing through the Hollywood Bowl.

"Nobody moves and nobody touches metal," came the calm deep voice of Lieutenant Steve Seidman.

The trio on stage froze in a drawing-room tableau as Seidman moved down the aisle between the seats and a pair of uniformed cops stepped in on either side of the stage.

"You followed me," I said.

"Phil thought it might be a good idea," he said.

"He was right."

The uniformed cops moved in, one on the stage to round up Wiklund and Jeffers, the other to take Stevens and his weapon.

"What was that crap about two people being dead?" Seidman asked, stepping next to me.

Bette Davis exited stage right.

"Made it up," I said. "I don't know where those guys are."

"Toby," Seidman said softly. "You are full of shit."

"Wait," Wiklund shouted from the stage, pulling out of the grasp of the policeman. "This isn't the way it's supposed to end. I simply won't tolerate another failure."

"Who hired you?" I asked.

"Never," he said suddenly, standing erect.

"Goddamn ham," Jeffers said behind him, trying to straighten up.

"Who hired you?" I asked Jeffers.

"How the hell do I know?" he answered. "King Lear here took care of everything. For all I know, he made the whole goddamn thing up."

"It's over," Bette Davis said, appearing at my side.

"Almost," I said.

"You are an enigma, Mr. Peters," she said. "And while Arthur and I are indebted to you, it is my fond hope that we never see each other again."

Seidman moved away from us toward the stage, from

which a broken Wiklund and a sagging Jeffers were being led.

"I've got one little thing you could do for me," I said.

"Besides having Arthur pay you?" she asked.

"Instead of that."

I told her what it was.

"And the recording? The real one of me and Howard Hughes?"

"I've got it someplace safe," I said. "If this didn't work out, I thought we might have to use it. I'm going to go break it and get a few hours' sleep."

"Thank you. Now, if you don't mind, I think I'd like to call my husband."

"Lieutenant Seidman will get you home," I said. "Don't forget tomorrow morning."

"Tomorrow morning," she said with a smile. "I will not forget."

Dash was sleeping in the Crosley. I didn't disturb him. I drove back slowly to the Farraday, thinking without thinking. I listened to Artie Shaw from the Aragon Ballroom in Chicago on the radio.

I had no trouble parking this time. It was late. My plan was to be sure that Alice and Jeremy hadn't gotten into any trouble helping me, and then to try to track down the person who had killed Niles, Pinketts, and Fritz. There was only one person it could be.

Fortunately, or unfortunately, I didn't have to put my plan to work. When I put my key into the outer door of the Farraday a figure spoke from the shadows.

"I've been waiting for you."

"How did you know I'd come back tonight?" I asked.

"Didn't, but I'm very patient and very determined," said Inez, showing me a gun that looked far too large for her hand but which she held with ease.

"And you want? . . ."

"The record," she said. "My mission is to get those plans

from Farnsworth. I believe that he will still be willing to trade them for his wife's reputation. My mistake, as you well know, was getting involved with that idiot Wiklund. I should have handled it myself from the start, but there are others who insisted... Please open the door and let's go inside."

I did what I was told. The lobby of the Farraday was dark except for the exit signs in the rear of the building and the single night-light on each floor.

"You killed Pinketts and Gray," I said.

"Ah, you found them. Well, their passing will not be mourned," she said. "Nor, I believe, will that of Grover Niles. Up the stairs."

"Can't make it up the stairs," I said. "Elevator."

"You found the incentive to overcome your agonies when we were in bed," she said.

"I was highly motivated. You want to take fifteen minutes going up? We'll walk."

"Elevator then," she said, and we got in.

We didn't say anything else until we got inside Shelly's office. The place was cleaner than I had ever seen it. Jeremy and Alice had done a great job.

"Where did you put it?" Inez asked.

"I didn't touch it," I said.

"The record," she said. "Now."

I turned toward her and scratched my head. "We've got a problem here, Inez," I said. "I give you the record and you kill me. It's going to be hard for me to believe anything else. So, I've got to come to the conclusion that if I'm going to die anyway, I might as well make it a bad day for you."

"I won't kill you," she said calmly.

"Why not?"

"I like you."

"Not convincing," I said.

"Do you have a suggestion?" she asked.

"You answer a question and I'll give you a plan." I tried moving to sit in Shelly's chair, the same chair in which

Andrea Pinketts had bought a scalpel in the neck from the lady in front of me.

"Ask."

"You killed Niles, Pinketts, and Stevens," I said.

"Yes, but that is not a question, and I've already as much as told you that I had."

"You work for the Nazis."

"Again, not a question," she said. "But technically incorrect. I am a Nazi—not a German, but a Bolivian. My family will be among those who bring a new National Socialist Party dominance to all of South America when the war is over. More questions?"

"No," I said. "That will be fine. John, you want to bring the record out for the lady?"

The door to my office opened and John Cawelti stepped in with a uniformed cop. Both had guns pointed at Inez. Cawelti also held a record in his hand.

Inez let out a little gasp and tightened her finger on the trigger.

"I'll blow your goddamn head off, lady," Cawelti said.

"He's a charmer, Inez."

"Lean over and put the gun on the floor and do it slow," Cawelti continued.

Inez leaned over and put the gun down. The cop moved quickly to pick it up.

"Where are the bodies, Peters?" asked Cawelti.

"I don't know, John," I said as Inez glared fire at me and said something fast in Spanish through clenched teeth.

"You're a lying son of a bitch," he said.

"But I'm not a killer," I reminded him. "You heard Inez confess, and Seidman has her helpers."

He walked over to me in the chair while the cop cuffed Inez.

"How did you know I was here?"

"Saw you come in earlier," I said. "Your car is still parked in front."

"This record," he said, holding it up. "What the hell is it and what was it doing under all those dishes in the sink?"

"Well," I said, getting up slowly, "I think it's . . ."

And my hand went out, hitting the record about in the middle of the label and sending it flying across the room and into the wall, where it shattered in a hail of black shards.

"You son of a bitch," Cawelti hissed, slapping me in the face.

I took it.

"Slipped," I said. "Sorry. It was Kate Smith singing 'God Bless America.'"

"The station, Peters," he said, his face going bright red. "Now. We're going to have a long, long talk."

Chapter Thirteen

Before I opened my eyes the next morning, I knew someone was standing over me.

The night before, Cawelti had personally taken my statement, making clear that he believed a little less than half of it. Some time after midnight and before dawn he let me go home. I'd made it to my room, yanked the mattress onto the floor, pulled off my pants and shirt, and crawled into bed without washing, shaving, brushing, or thinking. If I dreamed, I don't remember what my dreams were.

But I do remember the sense of dawn and someone over me.

I opened my eyes and looked up at a man in a neatly pressed gray suit and an old school blue-and-white tie. He was about forty, clean-shaven, with short auburn hair and no smile at all.

"Mr. Peters," he said.

"Yeah."

I tried to sit up or at least get my tongue to respond as he reached down with an open wallet. One side of the wallet held a small badge. The other side held a card which identified him as Special Agent Raymond Fielding of the Federal Bureau of Investigation.

"You been standing there long?" I asked, sinking back against my pillow.

"Not long, Mr. Peters," he said politely. "And I won't take much of your time."

"I'm in no hurry," I said, closing my eyes. "Have a seat."

"If you don't mind," said Fielding. "I'll stand."

"I don't mind."

"The Bureau has, through Federal Agency Proclamation 32.321, assumed jurisdiction over a highly classified investigation into an attempt to compromise the integrity of the United States by a foreign country with which we are at war. There is the possibility that three citizens of the United States were killed in connection with this attempt. The Bureau and its director would, in the interest of national security, prefer that all inquiries regarding this situation of national security be pursued exclusively by the Bureau."

"Which means?" I asked, blinking at him and rubbing the stubble on my face.

"The case does not exist," he said.

"Suits me just fine," I said.

"The director will be pleased to hear that. Assuming that you would, as have local law-enforcement agencies, agree to protect national security, I have been instructed to give you this."

He handed me a small brown envelope about the size and weight of a travel guide.

"Thanks," I said, putting the package next to my pillow. "What time is it?"

"Four minutes before eight," he said, without looking at his watch. "We trust that you will never discuss this investigation and your connection to it with anyone. Such discussion during wartime can be and will be considered a breach of the Sedition Act."

"You always talk like this?" I asked, trying to sit up again. He held out a hand to help me and I made it to my feet. "No," he said. "On my days off I drink a beer or two, go to football games when I can find them, and worry about my brother who's on a carrier somewhere in the Pacific."

"Thanks," I said, checking myself for the most tender remaining spots on my body. The odor was gone, but the aches were still there and raw.

Fielding reached down for the package he had brought, put it back in my hands, and left, closing the door behind him. I opened the package and found a neatly framed certificate of thanks for my contribution to safeguarding the freedom of the United States. The certificate was signed by J. Edgar Hoover. I put it on the dresser and climbed carefully into my pants.

I made it to the bathroom, shaved, washed, brushed my teeth, and leaned over to examine myself in the mirror. The hair on my chest was turning gray. My hair was still thick, though I could use a haircut, and my nose was still flat against my face and lacking in bone support.

"You are a mess, Tobias," I told myself, and that gave me the courage to go back to my room, have a glass of milk and some Hydrox cookies, and dress. I had one decent white shirt I had been saving—a birthday present from last November from Gunther—a two-by-two English broadcloth from Macy's that went for $2.19. My pants could have used a pressing and new pocket linings, but, all in all, I was almost presentable.

Mrs. Plaut was nowhere in sight and I made it to my car without a problem other than the shock to my ribs when I went down the front steps. Getting into the Crosley was no fun, but I made it, stopped at a flower stand on Hollywood Boulevard, and hit the hospital about eight-thirty.

Bouquet in hand, I made my way up to Ruth's room and started through the door before anyone could stop me. I stopped myself. Bette Davis was sitting next to Ruth, holding her hand and talking quietly. I let the door close part way and listened from the hall.

"I am deeply indebted to your brother-in-law and your husband," Davis said. "And I wanted very much to meet you."

"I can't believe this," Ruth said.

"Well," said Davis with great sincerity, "when I heard your name was Ruth, I felt a kinship. My real name is Ruth Elizabeth Davis. And my mother's name is Ruth."

"I know people say this to you all the time," said Ruth, "but I really am a fan. I can give you lines from *Dangerous, Marked Woman*, even *Satan Met a Lady*."

"Please," said Davis with a laugh. "If you spare me the memory of *Satan Met a Lady*, I will solemnly promise you a walk-on in my next film."

"No."

"Yes," said Davis, taking Ruth's hand in both of hers. "Promise. Get well and put on a few pounds and you will be on screen for posterity."

Ruth began to cry and I closed the door.

I sat on the chair outside the room with the flowers on my lap and made up my bill for Arthur Farnsworth. It came to a little over three hundred bucks, including gas, phone calls, doctor bills, bribes, socks, food, gas, pajamas, toothpaste, and daily charges. Before Bette Davis came out of the room, I tore it up.

When I heard the door open, I stood up.

"Thanks," I said, handing her the flowers.

"For me?" she asked. She was wearing a dark dress and a little hat with a hint of veil.

"For you," I said. "I've got another one coming for Ruth."

"I have in some ways misjudged you, Toby Peters," she said, leaning over to kiss my cheek.

"Mutual," I said.

"I like that woman," she said, gesturing with the bouquet toward Ruth's room.

"Me too," I said.

"I plan to keep in touch with her."

"Thanks," I said.

"And thank you," she answered, smelling her flowers.

A nurse coming down the hall recognized her and nudged another nurse who pointed to Bette Davis. Davis pretended not to notice and walked slowly, royally, to the elevator and out of my life.

In March, Ruth left the hospital. If you ever see *Hollywood Canteen*, look for her in the crowd scene doing the jitterbug with a gum-chewing sailor. She's the skinny smiling blonde in the white dress and the ribbon in her hair.

On August 23 that summer, a hot, humid Los Angeles day, Arthur Farnsworth was in town for a few days. He picked up a stole for Bette at Magnin's and then went to Hollywood to talk to Davis's lawyer, Dudley Furse, about a possible real-estate purchase.

As he walked past a cigar store carrying a briefcase, the owner and two customers heard a piercing scream and looked out of the window. They saw Farney fall straight backward, his head hitting the sidewalk. People rushed to help as Arthur Farnsworth went into convulsions, bleeding from the nose. His briefcase, which may have contained some of the secret work he was doing, couldn't be found.

Days later, the empty briefcase was returned to Bette Davis by a young boy who said he had found it half a block from the place where Farnsworth fell.

The autopsy report, which was lost soon after the inquest, included the statement by Assistant County Surgeon Homer R. Keyes, that, "A basal skull injury probably caused this man's death. It didn't result from the fall but instigated it." Keyes went on to say that the blow was probably caused by the butt of a gun or some other blunt instrument.

All this took place a few months after I got a call from Clark Gable, who wanted me to . . . but that's another story.